THE L(
CH1

b

Robbie Moffat

PALM TREE PUBLISHING

PALM TREE PUBLISHING
Paisley, Scotland Pa1 1TJ

© Robbie Moffat 2014-2019

First published in paperback JANUARY 2019

Typeset: Verdana 10pt

ISBN-10: 0 907282 74 1
ISBN-13: 9780907282747

PREFACE

Love and romance, action and adventure, the ingredients of good story telling. What the writer fails to tell us, we have to fill in for ourselves.

And so it is with The Loving Again, we take up where the story left us in another age, in a gone-world of yesteryear, when there was war and plague everywhere, and relationships were cut-short by death, illness and madness.

DEDICATION

This book is dedicated to Pat Trevor.
Rest in peace.

I see no end to man, no fall from paradise,
nor rise from hell. I see only flesh as atoms
of a cosmic energy, changing, rearranged,
to fit within the vessel of time, a swirling abyss
of solid void.

PART ONE

1

Great men and women rise out of the land just as quick as great men and women are buried in a hole in that self same ground. Sometimes, such greatness is recognised and rewarded, but most-times it is ridiculed, becoming shame and poverty, borne like a crucifix around the neck, until even it cannot protect the wearer from wrongs.

Likewise, it is the same with nations. History repeats itself like the tolling of a chapel bell; each ring may be louder than the last, or softer, but to the listener it is still the same dull, repetitive tone, cataloguing sin and announcing the pending moment for confession and redemption. At such moments, life becomes a matter of religion to those who suffer shame and poverty. It requires a leap of faith that does not want to be made by the great in wealth and influence, and without such a leap, nothing ever changes.

It is with this in mind that we come to Ireland in 1860, a nation seven hundred years under the yoke of the English, ploughing its earth for foreign masters; seeing its best sons slaughtered or exiled; making its best daughters ruined by childbearing and deprivation; having its children die of starvation. Yet, it was more than a problem of a standard of living. Admittedly, most Irish people lived near starvation level and depended upon one staple crop, the potato. With a population of eight and half million serfs, producing enough potatoes on one acre of land to feed a family of eight for a year, many who were able to work, left for England, the country responsible for their misfortunes. However, many more went to America where they became rich beyond their Irish imaginations, living at a level only the wealthy in Ireland could hope for.

In the eyes of many Irish people, though not all, poverty was not a problem, it was a disease inflicted on them by the English. The evils of Negro slavery in America were more easily canvassed in England than the miseries of the Irish serfs. The Irish serf, similar to his counter-part in Russia, lived by cultivating a plot of land on a nobleman's estate, paying rent for the land by giving his labour to his master for free. He was not bonded to the land, but there was too little land, and too many serfs. Nightly, they would all return to their mud huts or single-roomed cottages, for this was the habitation of Ireland, seven millions living in dwellings that were no better than when the English had first arrived seven hundred years before.

Therefore, it is with this at the forefront of our thought that we must view the events that were to divide a husband and wife for many years.

*

Patrick Trainor owned a moderate two story house in Killarney, Country Kerry where he practised law. He was happy living close-by Lough Leane, one of the three blue lakes of Killarney, a beauty spot much frequented by poets and clergymen. From the dining room window he had a clear view over the lough to Macgillycuddy's Reeks, the tallest mountains in all Ireland. To the left of them was Mangerton Mountain, an extinct volcano with its crater lake, the Devil's Punch Bowl, so deep that the water looked like black ink. It was said to be seven hundred feet deep, and it was believed that a childless woman longing for child who climbed the steep mountain and drank the icy water would have her wish.

Patrick had immense physical vigour and power of concentration. As a lawyer, he acted on behalf of land agents almost every day. He was a tall man, with fine, blue eyes, delicate hands, and a strong musical voice. His faults were obvious; there was coarseness in his Belfast manners, sharpness in his son-of-a-workman's tone, and roughness in many of his acts, above all, in his conversation. He became over-excited with his own voice, and although he was generally prudent and ready for compromise, his language often went beyond the bounds of decent attack. On the other hand, he was neither vindictive nor intolerant, but he was not afraid to speak his mind to his own people.

Patrick's father had been a tenant farmer from Mayo who had gone to work in the linen factories of Belfast. He had met his mother in the factory and married her shortly afterwards, and together they had made a comfortable home off Falls Road. Later, when his father had worked his way up to be under-manager in the factory, they moved to Holywood. They had not suffered the way other families had done during the famine, they prospered, and it was this prosperity that had bought Patrick a primary and secondary education. In Dublin he had studied with John Riley, a protestant from Waterford, and throughout their studies they had planned to go into practice together. They had picked Killarney because John had been there as a young boy and liked it, and ultimately because a practice became available with the murder of Robert Fitzharris, a lawyer embroiled in the landlord-tenant feuds.

It was while on business in Tralee that he had met the young red-headed Vivian O'Hara in a coffee-shop. He had fallen madly in love with her. She was twenty-one, he was twenty-four, and they married four months later on the day of the Greening.

2

Seven years later, Vivian was struggling to save her marriage. From the window of her bedroom Vivian had stared at Mangerton Mountain many times wondering if she would have to make the journey to the top. It was the mountains, just as much as the lakes, which attracted the English and Dublin folk so much, to the extent that during the summer months Killarney was overrun with English visitors taking refuge at the Royal Victoria Hotel and the many lesser establishments around the lake. The interest of the aristocratic tourist was predominantly riding and boating on the lakes, that of the middle-classes - visiting the ruined Castle, trekking to the Meeting of the Waters, then up Tomies Mountain if they had the stamina. Yet it was also the sun that brought them to Killarney, for it was the warmest place in the British Isles, and some years before, palms had been brought from Africa and planted in the public garden by the lake which already contained cedars of Lebanon, fuchsia, scented orchids, butterwort, and blue-eyed grass from Canada.

Patrick was still in bed and she was at her bedside table brushing her long red hair. She had a slight cough, she had always had a slight cough from her childhood. It was nothing serious, but sometimes damp air made it worse and she would cough throughout the night. She had caught a chill at the age of seven when she had gone to Dingle Bay with relatives and been allowed to spend too much time in the water. Since then she had always had a tickle in her lungs, nothing life threatening, but irritating enough in wet weather.

As she looked into the mirror she wondered where her twenty eight years had gone and screwed her nose up to see how many lines crossed her face, but there were none. She had never had a day's illness in her life, apart from the cough, and Doctor MacIntyre, when he had examined her, had told her she was the healthiest woman in

Killarney. She was in his words - a Kerry *cracker*.

Vivian Trainor, nee O'Hara, was medium-built, slim, and had fine facial features - high cheekbones and a thin delicate nose. She had a very thin waist, which even now she was a woman, was like a girl's. Yet, the rest of her, was well filled out, she was not skinny, she had strong muscular thighs that tapered to fine race-horse ankles; breasts that rose amply when she coughed, and an apple-shaped *derriere* that caught the eye of the many men in Killarney brave enough to steal a look. Vivian was vain enough to notice this, and it concerned her that her bottom might turn pear-shaped before she produced any children.

Vivian was no two-d picture of prettiness. She had strong beliefs. She was a spirited nationalist. She was a niece of the great Daniel O'Connell, the *Liberator* of Ireland, known to the people as *The Counsellor*, and she hated the way her husband Patrick took the part of the land agents over the tenants when it came to evictions. She told him so, for the shopkeepers in the town had grown progressively scornful when she used his 'eviction' money to buy goods. It made her extremely unhappy.

As she sat in front of the mirror, she thought back to when she was a child of seven. She had been happy then in her little pinafore dresses. She also remembered the year she caught the cough was the year the potato famine had started. The British had thought of sending to India for officials who were familiar with famines, but India was a long way off, and it was not until after the food depots had been set up that they arrived. By then it was too late. A million had died and since then two million had left for America. Now, it seemed there were very few young people left in Kerry and it was as though the people of the whole county were as old as Mangerton Mountain. She had even dreamt, that this was to be Ireland's future, a land of the old and the dying, until the English were out of Ireland forever.

Vivian put her brush on the dressing table in front of the mirror and went downstairs. It was summer, and as it was summer, she took in boarders so she would have some 'honest' money of her own to buy household items. She was an excellent host - she kept her hatred of the English in check until after the summer season was over. She prepared and presented the breakfast for her guests, three that morning, and as she cleared the table, she was asked the usual questions.

"Are there any leprechauns in Killarney?" one asked in a Yorkshire accent.

"To be sure" she replied in a strong Kerry burr, thicker than the butter she would get from the dairy "Why, this is the most terrible place in all Ireland for them!" She drew the words out, pronouncing *th* as *t* in the manner of the peasant folk. It irritated Patrick no end when he heard her speak like that, for in everyday speech, she had wonderful diction and a good turn of English phrase. "There was once a wicked Kerry land agent who wanted an old hunchback farmer to move out of the ruined castle so he could level the land for sheep. 'Not I' said the hunchback 'the leprechauns live here.' In reward for refusing to do as the land agent said, the leprechauns moved his hump to the land agent's back!"

Land agents took the brunt of Vivian's jokes, for she hated them with venom.

In all there were three male boarders that morning - a man in cotton from Leeds; a man in a boater and blazer from Middlesex who painted watercolours; and a gentleman dressed like a bohemian from Haselmere who was a poet. They were enjoying being entertained by the pretty lawyer's wife.

"How deep is the Devil's Punch Bowl, Mrs. Trainor?" the poet asked.

"The water's so deep" she said with the straightest of faces, the lines of concentration taut across her freckled face "there's no end to it at all. Last year, two young men went up the mountain to bathe, and after awhile, one noticed that the other was missing. So down the mountain he ran, fearing that his friend had drowned, and the rescue party dragged the Punch Bowl with ropes for a week, including Sunday, without finding the bottom. Then six months later comes a postcard from the drowned man saying he's arrived safely in Australia, and could he please send on his clothes. That's how deep it is ..." .

Patrick always told Vivian that it was the blood of the O'Connell's that made her talk that way, and that she should not jest with the guests and make them out to be fools. She said there was nothing in what she said, except a love of Ireland.

"Why don't you go and pull down the ivy creeping up the Abbey walls" she said angrily to Patrick afterwards when he had unbraided her for her remarks to the guests that morning "You should do something for Ireland." She was referring to the grey ghost of Innisfallen Abbey, were the last king of all Ireland, Brian Boru had been educated. For there was a saying that Ireland was the jewel of western Europe, that Kerry was the jewel of Ireland, that Killarney was the jewel of Kerry, and that the little uninhabited island of Innisfallen was the jewel of Killarney, and few would contest it. Now, half-hidden by shrubs, Vivian knew of no more perfect place than Innisfallen in which to spend a summer day. There was holy peace over it, but it distressed her to see the altar covered in green moss and the walls covered in ivy and deadly damp that would some day ruin it.

"You have too much passion for Irish things, past things, dead things, it's morbid." Patrick was jealous of his wife's flirtations with the boarders. He could see her slipping away from him. They needed something to bring them together again. "Let the stupid Abbey fall down and the land be used for something else. We need commerce, not trite little altars for tourists to visit, or wishing wells for them to throw their loose change into."

"Do you think a pony ride through the Gap of Dunloe is any better? Passion? Yes, I have a passion for Ireland. It's the truth, for I don't get any from you." She would no longer accept the blame for his lack of interest in sex. At first she thought that he no longer liked the way she looked, but the looks of other men confirmed that there was nothing wrong with her, that she was attractive, and desirable. "If I had a child, and a child I duly expect from you, I would bring it up to quit this land, for there is no future for any child of mine as long as Ireland is held back by landowners and lawyers like you doing the work of England in the name of Ireland."

It was the lack of a child more than anything that caused the arguments between Patrick and Vivian. They slept together in the same room, but in the true sense, they had not slept together for some considerable time, a common feature of middle-class marriages. Any love they had between them was fleeting; the marriage had turned cold, they had their separate interests, and apart from when they went to chapel on Sundays, she on his arm going in, and he on her's coming out, they rarely touched one another. Occasionally on parting, or at Christmas time when in view of their parents and other relatives, they would peck one another on the cheek as if to prove to the world that they were happy and that all was well with them. Of course, this was not so, they were both strong willed and opinionated. Neither would give in to the other's point of view; they had severe political arguments that would become rows - he firmly believed that Ireland had a place in the British Union, and as we know, she did not -

"We want the English to stay in England and keep themselves off the soil of Ireland. 'Tis only the fear of murder that keeps them from buying up every inch of God's country." She spoke with the Kerry brogue that irritated her husband. The vigour of the argument made her coughing worse. She did not want to argue with Patrick and go over and over the same ground, but as far as she could see, he was not even willing to concede any of his Unionist views. "I call it mob rule. It's hurting the economy and we're all the poorer for it." Patrick was incensed. He believed in the Emancipation Bill, in which Catholics had won the right to hold political office and trade freely, had gone a long way to making Irishmen equal with Englishmen. He stuck to that conviction despite the animosity it caused between himself and his wife. A better man might have hoped for a compromise, a coming to terms with political differences, and by doing so, side-step them, but not Patrick Trainor - he was principled, and loyal to the Queen - he had no time for his wife's stupid sentiments.

"Those mobs are good decent honest Irish folk driven to desperate action by landlords propped up by English investors - and backed up by Irish lawyers like yourself!" She shook her head so violently, her red hair, a legacy of the Viking blood passed down through generations of Kerry women, almost stood on end.

"Murder is murder, Vivian. You cannot negate that fact."

Vivian's green eyes flared red in an instant. "I don't want to negate anything but your blindness to what is going on in your own country. By Fianna, the day will come when we rise up and take what is ours." She began to cough incessantly, and she knew that she would soon be unable to argue any more even if she wanted to.

The mention of Fianna disturbed Patrick. This was a dangerous word on the lips of his wife.

"Who have you been talking to! Are you a Fenian?" He asked her directly without mincing his words.

"And what if I am?" she said clearing her throat.

"You better not have anything to do with this Stephens, I warn you?" Patrick almost poked his finger in Vivian's face. There was many a time he wanted to punch her fine-featured face, break her arrogant haughty nose, but he knew he never would. Instead, at times like this, he felt he should take her across his knee and spank that proud Irish bum she was always wiggling at other men, but that wasn't in him either. He felt lost, he did not know how to control his wife, how to make her do as she was told.

The whole of Ireland was looking for James Stephens who had escaped from prison. There were wanted posters everywhere. In the newspapers it stated that he was the leader of the Fenian brotherhood, a society backed by American money to overthrow British rule in Ireland and establish an Irish Republic. They had recruited members from the army and infiltrated the prison service.

It alarmed Patrick immensely.

"And what if I do know where he is?" replied Vivian with a throw of her head, knocking his hand away.

"Jesus Christ, Vivian, what are you getting yourself mixed up with now? If you've got anything to with his escape, you're done for. The rest of the Fenian's are being transported to Australia. Do you want to end up there?" He was genuinely upset "I won't follow on, you know."

"Oh be quiet, Patrick. You're like an old woman." Vivian hated to see a grown man, especially her husband, appear weak and pathetic in the face of her defiance. "If you were a man, then maybe Ireland would be a better place for us all."

Vivian burst out into a fit of coughing, and Patrick, seeing that his wife's one weakness was not a thing he could take advantage of, fetched her some water. Thus their argument ended, for the differences between the Trainors were too wide to bridge in a morning. Neither approved of the other, and after seven years the marriage had become a sham.

3

Vivian had taken up an interest in nationalist politics; attending meetings, marching on demonstrations, organising collections for pamphleteering. She would regularly make the long journey by carriage to Mallow and catch the train to Dublin. She was in her element, and as the niece of

O'Connell the 'The Liberator', she was in great demand to speak at meetings and to be included in the secret gatherings that were taking place everywhere.

A few days after their morning argument, she told Patrick she was off to Cork for the night to see her sister Mary. The journey to Cork was the same old journey by coach it had always been, one in which she caught up sleep from the early seven o'clock start, and which got her into the city a little before midday.

Vivian did not go to her sister's; for that is not the reason she had journeyed to Cork. Instead she was to meet a man on the South Gate Bridge as pre-arranged. She clutched in her hand a little pack of shamrock seed attached to a postcard. This was the means by which she would be distinguished by the 'brother' who had been told to look out for a girl with red hair. She stood, as she was told, over the keystone at the centre of the bridge.

The lunchtime crowd was moving along, the women distinctive, with their black shawls over their heads like mill-girls, some of the woman as dark as their shawls - the legacy of the Spanish wine-trade blood that ran thick in the people of Cork. Suddenly, the wheel of a donkey cart flew off and clattered along the cobbles. A howl of laughter went up, as a shocked cart owner chased his rolling wheel across the bridge.

Vivian smiled and exchanged nods and comments with passers-by amused by the sight. She continued to wait. A young bare-footed girl came up and asked her for a farthing, but she sent her on her way empty-handed.

She hated to see children begging, she always had, and she always would.

A crowd had gathered around the cart. The old man to whom the cart disaster had happened was apparently a familiar character. The crowd appeared to know him well. When he saw that his trouble was causing amusement, he decided to make the most of his audience, and of the situation. He began by speaking to his donkey, a woefully calm, yet completely stupid beast, relating to it how the road had been uneven, the load over heavy, the cart wheel past its best, the bridge steep, the donkey too slow, and that by a combination of these factors, the wheel had decided it could cross the bridge all by itself easier than attached to the cart.

The crowd howled and clapped, and Vivian momentarily forgot why she was there at all. She clutched the postcard in her hand and it crumpled and rolled into a tube as she nervously played with it. She turned from the crowd and looked down into the waters of the Lee and thought that over the laughter and bustle she could hear the bells of Shandon. 'Now, wouldn't that be grand' she thought, when suddenly, a hand was thrust before her face, holding a postcard and a packet of shamrock seeds. She turned.

It was James Stephens! He was the man she was to help? The man she was to pretend to be married to for an afternoon? Vivian nearly fainted, but she caught hold of herself, walked to the end of the bridge with him, where he flagged down a hackney carriage. He was carrying a small pack case.

"Monkstown" he told the cabman. He had a deep, refined, voice, and as Vivian got in beside him she noticed his strong muscular hands, unlike Patrick's hands which had never picked up anything heavier than a pen. She could not see his eyes, they were hidden under the brim of a cloth cap, and she could see little of his face because the collar of his coat was turned up, but she knew it was Stephens all right.

"Getting out" said the cabman with a backward glance.

Stephens said nothing. His right hand reached into his coat.

"To be sure, I don't blame you", said the cabman. "Didn't a daughter of mine go last week with her husband sailing for New York. Sure, I've another daughter already there in Tyrone, Pennsylvania. It breaks me heart, so it does."

It was a half-hour journey over the hills to Monkstown on the coast. Nothing else was spoken during the journey. Stephens relaxed a little once he could smell the sea air. Vivian sat beside him occasionally stealing glances at him. She found it hard to believe that this was the man half the police force in Ireland was looking for. If they caught him he would be sent to do twenty years hard labour in Australia; perhaps they might even find a reason to hang him. And what would they do to her? And Patrick? He'd be finished with the law, for sure. She coughed.

Stephens took her hand, and the application of pressure from his grip made the control of her coughing easier.

"Easy now, my girl" he spoke in a deep tone. The sound of his voice made Vivian stop coughing. She could feel his power, and she felt attracted to it, overwhelmed by it. There was an energy emitting from him that made her tingle. She began to imagine that she had run away from Patrick and that she was going away with this man, a complete stranger, to start a new and wonderful life. The miseries of Killarney had been left behind from the moment she had met him on the bridge. Feelings that had been submerged for years came percolating out of her, and desires, deep sexual desires which had been repressed by neglect and indifference, re-surfaced in the instant he had taken her hand. For the first time in as long as she could remember, she felt like a woman, she felt like making love, with the man holding her hand.

She leant into his arm and smelt the smells of a dozen places unknown to her. The coarseness of his jacket was like velvet to her empty life of housekeeping and meal making. A cough rose, but she smothered it by burying her nose into his shoulder where it seemed to remain forever. She took his hand and placed between her breasts, then slowly, ever so slowly, guided his hand down across the flatness of her abdomen and into the folds of her dress between her thighs. He did not resist as she encouraged him to explore the inside of her thighs by rocking her head on his shoulder, rising higher and higher until her lips reached for the flesh of his neck, her free arm now across his chest and around the back of his neck and into his hair, wanting all the time for him to reach down and kiss her on the lips.

She was like a schoolgirl, and were it not for the shortness of the journey, the openness of the hackney, and arrival at Monkstown, she might have given way to complete abandonment of self-control. For due to reasons unknown even to herself, she had been affected and aroused by this man she had only just met, in a way she had read about, but which until then, she had never believed possible. She felt no shame or guilt, she felt that for once she was following her feelings, acting them out in a way that had not been possible in Killarney. After all, she was this man's 'wife' for the afternoon, and to anyone who might be watching, they were behaving as man and wife ought to behave.

Monkstown was busy with travellers. The cabman drew up at the hackney post by the ferry pier. He did not draw away from her. Without a word, he stole a kiss, the kiss of a strong powerful man, not the weak ineffectual peck of a husband tired of his wife and thinking of his work; no, it was the kiss of a man in control.

As their lips parted, he laughed a little, the first, and only time she saw him laugh. He had a beautiful broad smile and straight white teeth. The skin around his eyes became a sea of little lines, and the irises of his dark eyes, looked into her like no man had ever done, pierced straight to the bottom of her heart and saw her yearning for love. Yet, he was not laughing at her, he was laughing with her, for she too was smiling from having been kissed unexpectedly, knowing that her advances had not been rejected.

He leant forward, paid the cabman, sprung out the cab, turned, and lifted Vivian out of the carriage with his strong hands. He put her on his arm and led her down to the ferry that crossed over to Cork Harbour on Great Island where the emigrants embarked on the daily steamers. She had no idea which ship he would be catching, but she could see the harbour was full of steam ships and tall masters. As yet she could not see the quay, but as she disembarked from the ferry with Stephens and the host of passengers laden with their belongings, and walked the short mile over the crest of the island tip, there below was Queenstown, the saddest place in all of Ireland, thronging with people, baggage, goods - not a length of the quay free of the tenders that carried the emigrants out to the waiting ocean-going ships.

She stood clinging to Stephen's arm witnessing hundreds of emigrants embark in the tenders for the New York bound masthead merchantman from Falmouth. An immense crowd had gathered to bid them a long goodbye. Vivian found it impossible to witness the exodus without heart-pain and tears. A mother hung on to the neck of son; a young girl clung to an elder sister; an old white-haired father fell on his knees, arms uplifted, and implored the Almighty to protect his departing children. One old woman in front of Vivian was sobbing on the shoulder of a middle-aged man.

"Thomas! Thomas! All's gone from me in the wide world when you're gone! You were all I had left, the last of me seven sons! Oh, Thomas, Thomas, never forget your mother - your mother, Thomas, your poor old mother, Thomas!" The old woman was beside herself.

Thomas, his gray hair caught by the afternoon sun, supported his mother in his arms until she fainted, then he lifted her into a small carriage that conveyed his baggage to the quay, and kissed a weeping young woman who was leant against the horse.

"I'll send home for you both next year, Peggy, I promise I will" he said wringing her hands in his own "and you'll be child to me Ma from this out till then, and then you'll be me own."

Stephens tugged Vivian by the arm, and when she looked around again, the middle-aged man had gone; Peggy had wound her arms around the old woman while a young girl held a broken cup of water to the old woman's lips.

Vivian was led through the din, the noise, the people pressing and rolling in vast masses towards the place of embarkation like the waves of the troubled seas they would cross. Men, young and old, were embracing each other and crying like children. Vivian noticed a number of them carrying treasured relics from their villages to remind them of home - a small branch of sweet blossoms and green leaves of an already withered hawthorn; a bunch of meadowsweet. Shrieks and prayers, blessings and lamentations mingled in one great cry from those on the quay, and those embarking on the tenders for the New York ship, were likewise infected by the cries of those waiting to depart on an Australian bound ship.

There was very little ceremony to get in the tenders. Stephens paid for his passage in English pounds and kissed Vivian on the lips.

"God Save Ireland." he whispered in her ear. He took a step back, picked up his small pack case, and turned to descend into a tender.

In an impulse, just as he was about to leave off the quay, she took his hand and thrust a small piece of stone into his hand. He stared at what she had given him.

"A piece of Innisfallen" she stated proudly "to remember the old country by."

Stephens dropped into the tender clutching his piece of Ireland, and as the last man in, he untied the painter and pushed it clear of the quay. He continued to stand upright as the oarsmen began to pull through the waters of the harbour towards the steamer.

"God Save Ireland!" she shouted over the hubbub on the quay, and she watched until she saw the tender reach the steamer. She saw Stephens go aboard. She remained on the quay while a father sprinkled an old couple with holy water and they crossed themselves; until at last, after an hour's delay, with the sound of St. Patrick's Day being played in the fo'castle on a whistle and a big drum, the ship raised anchor. Slowly, but steadily, the ship passed between Spike Island and Whitegate Bay, where Vivian lost sight of it from the cliffs as it went out beyond Roches Point, into the deep swell of St. George's Channel and the Atlantic Ocean.

*

Vivian had been aroused so much by her meeting with Stephens, she had not gone to her sister's, but to a hotel room in Queenstown where she had lain on the bed and repeatedly relieved her longing. The feel of the sheets against her naked body, the circulation of the sea air between her legs and across her haunches, heightened her arousal to a fever, as she explored her own body the way she wished to be explored by a man, but had never been by her husband.

In the end she cried herself to sleep. It terrified her that she had such sexual desires, the touching of her own body had taken her on a more erotic journey than the flesh of her husband had ever taken her; the curves of her own body an exploration over virgin territory. No-one had ever spoken to her about the pleasures to be discovered with the body, the female body, her body. Twenty eight years had gone by, and she had never until then, experienced such a sensation, such an overwhelming numbness, that had first made her cry with pleasure, then lulled her into such a calm that she could not move. The scent that accompanied the numbness was new to her, she had never thought that she could produce such a sweet sticky substance, or that the small region she had discovered was the source of it. And it was the chance discovery of the tender area in the folds of her most private parts that came as her greatest joy, as first the pleasure, then the regret of not having discovered it when she was a pubescent girl, made her weep, and subsequently, led her to cry herself to sleep at recognition of her own ignorance.

4

Patrick, sickened by his wife's uncompromising nature, had taken to going out in the evening. It was a natural thing for a man to do when his wife had not produced any children after seven years. He partly rued the fact that he had married Vivian O'Hara, for she was a shrew of a woman who he could not control. He had heard it whispered in his ear many a time, by his partner John Riley that he should take a belt to her backside, but he had told Riley that it was not in his nature to hit a woman, even if it was his wife.

Between them, John Riley and Patrick Trainor had built up a law practice that was doing nicely. They were both hard workers who made light of their skills, and the gentry used their services time and time again as their legal affairs were dealt with quickly and efficiently. More importantly,

Riley & Trainor got results when dealing with evictions, and this more than any other kind of case, brought the money rolling in, for evictions meant increased re-letting rents for landlords, and, good profits when the land was re-sold to investors.

However, dealing with the evictions of tenants was not without its perils, and Patrick Trainor had become accustomed to taking his manservant O'Donaghue, and Riley's younger man called Sullivan, a brute of a fellow, along with him on out of town journeys that involved evictions. There had been a number of beatings, and on two occasions, the murder of landlords who had evicted tenants, but as yet, no one had turned their ire on Trainor or his partner Riley.

Patrick was taking no chances. He had his job to do, and if that meant he had to employ bodyguards, then the client would pay for it. Riley had carried a new eviction order in the district of Tralee through the courts and the landlord had asked Patrick to enforce it. It involved the eviction of a large number of tenants from land under the lee of the Stack Mountains. In all there were about twenty tenants who had fallen behind on their lease-rents; they had refused to pull down their fences (the stone dikes separating the land into smallholdings), and banded together, taking it into their heads that the land should be the focus of national agitation and action against rule from Westminster.

Patrick suspected that the Fenians had stirred the tenants up, and that amongst

them was a man who was the ringleader.
And indeed there was - a man called Duffy
who had whipped up the tenants into
believing that they had improved the soil
with their labour, not the landlord, and that
as they had added to the value of the land,
they should be paid compensation. They,
the tenants, had built the cottages in which
they lived, and by rights should not be
evicted from what was rightly their
property.

The tenants were angry and hostile when
Patrick arrived with his two men, the
landlord's bailiff, and a squad of police
armed with rifles, bayonets, and hand-
cuffs. They swelled out of their crofts and
gathered by the stream at the place where
the women worked their washing. Patrick
spoke from his horse:

"You are hereby, by order of the
magistrates court in Killarney, to quit these
dwellings and leave this land forthwith ...."

or words to that effect, for none could hear
what Patrick Trainor was saying due to the
insults and blaspheming being directed at
him and his police escort.

Duffy stepped forward. "You are a traitor to
Ireland, Patrick Trainor, and to be sure,
you'll rot in hell before I will."

"Your system, Duffy, rots whole
communities. You band together a few
outcasts and make them take illegal course
that makes everyone else's life a misery.
Your deliberate association with these
peasants ensures the outrage of every
civilised man from here to Dublin. These
people will now face utter destitution and

abandonment. For what end? To bring anarchy and insurrection upon us?"

Gavin Duffy was a small bald-headed man with a round face and small eyes, committed to the cause of a Free Ireland despite the poverty and ruined personal life it had brought him.

"Justice, Patrick Trainor" Duffy replied. "In England tenants are protected by the law and repaid if they add value to the land, but not in Ireland. Why?" He drew his attention to the tenants.

Patrick, shifted a little on his saddle as he surveyed the poor farmers he was helping to evict. In total, there were about forty men, young and old; about the same number of women similar in age range as the men; and around ninety children, many still babes in arms. Together, their twenty smallholding's covered the hillside of a small glen that led up into the mist of the Stacks. The community had been there for generations, and they had supplemented their simple crop growing by grazing sheep and goats on the high moors. Most of the women and children were bare-footed, but this was nothing out of the ordinary.

"It's Irishmen like you, Patrick Trainor, that's sickened me of me own country. I'm off to Australia, and there's many here, who'll follow me there. There's none here who'll take an axe-handle to yer armed coppers just to see themsel's transported to Australia when they could sail from Limerick themsel's as freemen. You can have your sick old mother Ireland for yerself and yer robbing landlords. Continue to have yer way, and there'll be none left in Ireland to rent the land to. The land is yours, take it."

With that final statement, they set fire to their own dwellings and Gavin Duffy led the community off the slopes of the Stacks like some Moses in the deserts of Egypt. Every single last man, woman and child, picked up their few packed possessions, and followed Duffy without uttering a word. They filed past Patrick Trainor without a glance of recognition, except for a young girl, barelegged, scantily dressed, about seven years of age, carrying a rag doll under her arm. She looked at Patrick with eyes that he had seen before, but where? He could not place the look. Then, as her mother tugged her hand, and she was forced to look away, with horror, Patrick recalled the eyes of Christ Redeemer in the cathedral in Dublin. The look from the eyes of that statue had always terrified him - 'I died for your sins' the words below the effigy's blood stained feet pinned to the cross.

How could a little peasant girl imitate such a look? As a boy he had been an exceptional scholar, one of the first Catholics to be admitted to Trinity, but as a catholic he was not eligible for scholarships or prizes, and his fees and support money had been paid by family members who had emigrated to America.

Now, thirteen years later, at the age of thirty-one, sitting on his horse in the lee of the Stack Mountains, he felt nothing. It was a dog eat dog world, and as far as he could see, most people would never stop believing that the world owed them a bone. People like Duffy tried to change things to suit themselves, but they were working outside the law trying to make the law conform to what they thought it should be. It was the cart before the donkey, and it would never work. The only way to change the system was from the inside. If, like his partner Riley, who had been admitted to the bar, he put the law before his religion, it was said in higher places that he would be favoured better. Patrick knew what that meant, and was all for it, but first, there was the little matter of facing his wife, and telling her that he wanted to become a protestant.

Once the business with the farmers was over, and he had reported to the landlord the success of the day's business, he had made up his mind that he would convert to the protestant faith, no matter the protestations he would suffer from his wife.

*

Patrick returned to Killarney the following day. He had had terrible dreams in the night and returned in the morning dejected and depressed to remember that Vivian had gone to her sister's in Cork. He found himself alone in the house, tired and lonely. He went to bed for awhile and rose about six o'clock. He did not expect Vivian back until late the following evening, so as usual in such situations, he thought of going to the Royal Victoria for some dinner. He went up to change out of the clothes he had slept in, but he could not find any clean underclothes in his cabinet. Thinking there may have been a mix up, he opened his wife's drawers one by one, and somehow, it is not always clear how these things happen, he found himself trying on his wife's undergarments. He paraded in front of her dressing table mirror admiring himself, and found to his surprise, that it aroused him sexually. It was a dangerous discovery.

*

Vivian caught Patrick cross-dressing when she came home early the following evening from Cork. It was innocent enough - he was wearing one of her undergarments and looking at himself in front of the mirror in the hallway. At first she thought that she had caught him on his way to bed from having undressed in the kitchen, and that on hearing the door open, he had taken whatever garment had come to hand and put it on. However, further thought eliminated this notion as slowly she came to realise that what he was wearing had come from one of her drawers upstairs in the bedroom.

"You will take that off right now!" she shouted at him. She had come home with the hope of talking to her husband about her own discovery, and sharing with him, and perhaps even encouraging him to explore her in new ways that the previous seven years had not revealed. Now, suddenly, with the realisation that her husband wore women's clothes, she was devastated. Patrick obeyed her and handed the under-garment to her.

"Tomorrow, Patrick, you will go to Father Connor and tell him about this." Patrick had nodded his head. "You will sleep in one of the boarder rooms tonight. I will tell the Father why I haven't had a child yet, for he's asked me before, and I let him think it was me, not you. I don't have anything else to say to you right now."

Vivian took the under-garment, a white chemise petty-coat, went upstairs, lit a fire, and burnt it. Then, she lay on the bed, not daring to think any more about it. She could hear Patrick come up the stairs and go into one of the spare rooms. She waited awhile then undressed and got into bed naked, a thing she had never done before the previous afternoon in Queenstown. She lay a long while in the hope of going to sleep, but her time with Stephens, the discoveries of the night before, the feelings of fulfilment, the sensations that followed, led her once again to explore the curves of her breasts, the fullness of her hips, the heat of her inner thighs, until at last, with her back arched, and the bedclothes kicked to her ankles, she experienced full female pleasure in her own bed for the first time. Later, she thought of Patrick and began to cough, and cough repeatedly, until she covered her nakedness with the bedclothes and finally went to sleep.

*

Vivian waited outside the confession box until Patrick had told Father Connor about his mixed up feelings. He emerged with a sheepish grin that hid his humiliation. She glared at him and entered the confessional herself. At last, it seemed that any doubt about her being barren had been laid aside by Patrick's confession, for the Father absolved her of all blame in the marriage, though he reminded her that in the eyes of God, they were man and wife until death did them part.

Vivian did not tell the Father about her intimacies with Stephens or herself. After all, he was a man, and he would view her actions as adulterous, and her pleasures with herself as sinful. Vivian felt she had done nothing wrong, that what she had done with Stephens was for the cause of Ireland, and what she did to herself in her own bed was her own secret.

Patrick continued to sleep in the spare room, and she, left to experimentation, began to sleep better than she had for a long time.

6

Using the humiliation of talking to Father Connor as an excuse, Patrick converted to being a Protestant. He tiraded on about the Catholic Church and the monies sent to Rome. More than anything, he blasted the church for its iconography and ritual, and went on for half-an-hour about abuses priests made of the confessional box. But in the end, he let it slip to Vivian that it would advance his career better.

Vivian's contempt for his conversation was almost as great as her contempt for his sexuality. In her eyes he was a *souper* - his religion bought by the British in return for favour with the Unionists.

The outward result was that Vivian had to go to the chapel every Sunday alone, Patrick no longer on her arm, but he did not give damn. For his part, he saw his practice thrive. He had become the leading lawyer in the district for eviction cases, and as a champion of the landed, he began to move in social circles he had not enjoyed previously as a Catholic. He happily lived with the spitting and abuse he received in the streets of Killarney and its outlying villages, his income increasing enormously, to the extent that he was quickly in a position to buy a grander house with a piece of adjoining land.

However, his wife, married to a *souper,* found herself shunned by the very nationalists she had encouraged to take up the fight. Despite what she had done for Stephens, Vivian's influence in their circles waned almost overnight, and having no income of her own bar the summer boarders, she found that she was tied to her husband for financial reasons whether she liked it or not.

Inside herself, Vivian renounced any love she had for Patrick, but for appearances, she remained in the house with him. When it came to move to the larger house situated right on Lough Leane, she moved with him, for despite her detestation of his ideals and morals, she was his wife, and she had nowhere else to go. She thought of emigrating to America, just up and offing

one fine autumn morning, but she could not
bring herself to quit the country she loved
so dearly. She thought that she could go to
her sister in Cork, but she had five children
and a husband who drank, and lived in a
terrace house with only three rooms. She
thought to return to her mother and father,
but that was admitting defeat, and she was
proud, too proud to admit that Patrick
Trainor had got the better of her.

Patrick, however, was still in love with
Vivian. It was a freak of nature, or perhaps,
he thought, divine intervention that made
him what he was. God had not done him
any favours making him as he was, and
began to blame his catholic upbringing for
his inadequacies. But there was nothing he
could do about it, he was attracted to men
however hard he tried to deny it to himself.
He would see a young man by the lake,
fresh from Trinity or Oxford, and be drawn
to him in the manner Socrates was drawn
to the young men of Athens. He would
befriend them, but he would go no further
than conversation or an early evening drink
in the Royal Victoria, always returning at a
respectable hour to his own home and
Vivian.

She would not wait for his return, she
would engross herself in Irish history and
lore, collect flora or tend the vegetable
garden she painstaking encouraged to grow
for the sake of her own health, rather than
that of her husband's.

Patrick had taken on O'Donague and his
wife as house servants. Shaun O'Donaghue
was from Limerick, and as well as

accompanying his master on evictions, he attended to all external house matters such as repair, general garden pruning, lawn cutting, wood cutting, and the care of the master's two horses which he used for his business in the outlying districts. He also groomed Vivian's trap-pony, Volcano, so named after Mangerton Mountain because of his volcanic looks and devil's temper;

"Now, Volcano" Vivian would scold him "if you act up today, I'm going to have you drowned in Castlelough Bay."

Volcano was her closest companion, a fifteen-year-old horse that had been bought from a tinker coming from Cork. She loved him, she adored him the way mother's adored their children; she fussed over him, and if the weather was bad, she would refuse to take the trap out in case Volcano caught horse cough or any other sort of ailment brought on by exposure to the Irish elements. She never thought of her own cough, and would not think twice about taking the wolf-hounds she kept as guard-dogs out walking in the same inclement weather that Volcano was not allowed out in.

The maidservant, Shaun's common law wife, Colly, was a fifty-five year old widow who Shaun had met in Connemara some years before. It was she who made the meals and cleaned the house now that the Trainor's had moved to the big house and no longer took in boarders.

To Colly, her mistress was brooding, and she questioned her a few times as to why she had no children yet, for she knew nothing about her master's nature, except that he was a *souper*, something which was of no concern to her or her husband as neither of them went to church.

"Here, miss" Colly said one night while master Patrick, having taken Shaun with him, was away on business "I've been tinking ....." She was sitting in front of the big room fire on a wooden chair knitting for her husband while her mistress was reclined in a leather armchair beneath a candelabra reading a copy of Fitzgerald's *Rubaiyat of Omar Khayyam*.

"What was that, Colly?" she asked without looking up.

"'Tis wee 'uns you should be having, miss Vivian, not nights with poets."

"Not that again, Colly." Vivian had almost cut off thoughts about having children. She was twenty-eight, and feeling forty.

"I be thinkin' meself, a climb up Mangerton Mountain be what's need'd, miss. Mellia murther, a fine coleen like ye should be havin' ten bairns. See wouldn't ye get a bairn' doin' that." she said as if Mab, Mother Ireland had come to her in a blaze of light and bestowed wisdom on her. "In a house as big as a cassel as well, ye have, an not the sound of a little one, so help me." Colly wanted to break into the Gaelic to express herself in a way that her young mistress might not take offence, but there was so much English spoken nowadays, thought Colly, and it was better, and more proper, that she heard the truth from her in the language of the gentry. "Ye'll be hearin' it from meself, me lass, the way of it is,

that th' watter up ther' as powers ....."
Coleen O'Donaghue had produced ten children - Mary had died at childbirth, Maureen had been killed in a horse accident, and her three other daughters had been lost in Cholera epidemic of '32. All her boys, according to herself, were all built like oxes - Joseph was in the British army; Michael and Thomas had gone to California for the gold rush of '49; Peter was a seaman on a tramp-ship; and her youngest James, had enlisted in the Union army in America to fight slavery but hadn't been heard of since the second Battle of Manassas in '62.

"'Tis nonsense, Colly O'Donaghue, and you know it" Vivian dismissed her about Mangerton Mountain. "'Tis time an old woman like you is in bed before the banshees get you."

"Aye, 'tis late, an ' me ol bones are creakin' like the boards on th' floor. Good night, miss Vivian" Colly rose from her chair, taking her knitting with her, shuffling across the bare polished floor of the big room in her Indian slippers, a present from her eldest son Joseph, a sergeant serving under General Rose's command in India.

She closed the door behind her, and Vivian listened to her going down the corridor of the hall to the back of the house and the servant's quarter.

Vivian dropped her book and brooded by the fire until the embers started to glow. 'Yes' she thought to herself Mangerton Mountain? Why not?' There and then she decided she would climb the mountain the following day, weather permitting, and if nothing else, the exercise would do her good.

*

Vivian rose at six. It was a glorious sun filled day. There was not a cloud in the sky. She took her horse and trap beyond Muckross Abbey and Torc House, and left her beloved animal feeding by the Owengarriff River, a mile above the Torc Cascade, a little before eight.

She started the ascend of the mountain in a pair of breeches and wide winter weather coat, for although there was a blue clear sky and not a breath of wind, it was February and in the shade of the valleys there were pockets of low lying mist and frost. She wore kid gloves and a woollen hat, but soon the exertion made her hot, and she discarded both, putting them into a satchel she had slung over her shoulder.

She had not been on the mountains for almost two years, the last occasion with some of her boarders who had invited her for a picnic on Torc Mountain, but when she had been younger, she and Mary had regularly climbed the Stacks and the Slieve Mish, and one adventurous summer, scaled Brandon Hill, the fourth highest mountain in Ireland.

Now, after years of indolence, she was finding the going tough, but once on the track that led to the top, she was determined to scale Mangerton's two thousand seven hundred feet. As she climbed, the air became cooler and the heat of the sun weaker, until feeling the rise of a northerly breeze, she replaced her hat and gloves, and struggled on. She rested every three hundred feet, and about two thirds of the way up, stopped to drink some tea she had brought in a vacuum flask.

She was now almost level with the lowest peaks of the MacGillicuddy range, and began to see for the first time, patches of snow in hidden north-facing hollows. Nearer, and below her, were the Upper Lakes glistening in the sun, ribboning their way north and down into Muckross Lough, and ultimately into Lough Leane. The beauty of it was so inviting, Vivian consumed it with her eyes for as long as she could, wishing she had one of those new photograph boxes she'd seen boarders use.

She rose and puffed and coughed the rest of the way up the mountain, until just a little before eleven o'clock, she crested the rim of the black-cliffed cauldron and saw a little way below where she was standing, the black waters of the Devil's Punch Bowl.

She felt exhilarated. All the times she had answered her boarders questions about the Punch Bowl with tongue in cheek without ever having seen the waters herself - there at last was the secret of Mangerton Mountain - a body of water so still and so deep that for all she knew it truly might have gone right through the centre of the Earth and come out in Australia.

Vivian was not naturally superstitious, no more so than any other Irish woman, but there were in Ireland whose who did not believe in leprechauns, and those who did not, were heathens. Folklore was so much a part of Kerry culture, that at times it was difficult to separate legend form history, fact from heresy, fairies from fools. For all she knew, there may just be something in the water of Mangerton Mountain that was like no other water and helped a woman to be fertile. Was it not a fact that the Madonna statue at Clonmel shed blood as tears?

Vivian approached the water and at its edge looked into it but saw nothing, not even her own shadow. She took out the flask from the satchel and poured out the tea on to shoreline stones. She filled the flask.

"So" she said aloud "if you be listening, whoever you are, I be wanting me a child. I won't be caring who the father is, and for sure, the father won't be caring to know if it's his or not, but I want a child, and I'll have it." With that, she drank some of the icy water, and if felt good, for she was very thirsty after the long climb. She drank some more, and drank enough until she felt that there was no mistaking that she had drunk from the Devil's Punch Bowl.

The deed was done, she thought, 'All I need to do now is to find a man to father the child.'

*

Patrick returned home early with Shaun soaked to the skin. The day had started out so promising and ended with the return of sleet and snow, then gale, which carried rain in from the Atlantic.

Colly fetched the two men towels and dry clothing and they all sat together in front of the kitchen fire drinking hot toddies. Patrick lounged with his feet perched on the grate the two hounds at his chair, and had Colly not scolded him, he would have burnt the fine woollen socks she had knitted for him.

"Where's Mrs.Trainor?" he asked Colly after awhile.

"What? I tought the missus went with ye to Mister Riley's this morn, so she did."

"Did you see the mistress this morning, Shaun?" he asked O'Donahgue with a poke in the arm, for he had fallen asleep in his chair.

""What's that your sayin', sir. I was away with the fairies." O'Donaghue rubbed his eyes. He was not as young as he used to be, and he took naps whenever he could to make up for the early rises.

"Did you see Mrs.Trainor this morn?" he asked again

"Saw her go off wi' Volcano about haf-six." He was used to his master checking up on his wife, for it was well known amongst the town men that he was jealous of anyone even looking at her. This time though, O'Donaghue saw something-else, a look of concern he never thought his master could have for his wife. "It was still dark, but the sky was clear, and the light was good." His master was looking for more information from him. "To be sure, when I tink about it now, when I put the horses to feed when we came back, I missed seeing Volcano."

"Now, me young sir, don't ye be gettin' fuming" interceded Colly, for she was well aware of their sleeping arrangements "The missus be a fine wife to ye, and she'll be back soon enough, swear to god, weather permittin'."

The rain rattled against the windows of the kitchen and Patrick sat brooding at the fire imagining that his wife had run off to live with another man. He had been rotten to her. He had given her everything she wanted before they were married - flowers, gifts, little love notes, even written a poem - but from the moment they were married he had put his work before her; said he was too busy for love-making when she had flung her arms round him; found work reasons not to take her to Cork or Dublin; discouraged visits from her relatives and friends; ridiculed her in front of boarders; criticised her about how she dressed, how she looked, how she behaved; in general, made her life a misery. Why? To be left alone in a house with two old servants who could hardly string a sentence of English together. Is this what he had lived almost thirty-two years for? A big house? Two fine horses? Friendships with the gentry? It meant nothing, it all meant nothing without someone to share with, without someone to love and achieve these things for. All his achievements, his moneymaking, the servants, the house - all of it had been for Vivian.

"Are you sure nothings happened to her?" Patrick asked his servants. "Colly, you spoke to her last night before she went to bed. Did she say where she was going today?"

"Now, master, it be a hard ting to remember yesterday from tomorrow, m'tinks at me age." Colly thought for a moment. "We'se be talkin' bout bairns, I remember's tat .... and 'bout Mangerton Mountain."

Patrick knew the legend well. "She didn't go up there today, did she?"

A look of horror crossed Colly's wrinkled old face. "Ye's not be tinkin' ...." She started to rummage in the kitchen dresser.

"She n'er take Volcano out in tis rain" added O'Donague "'Tis not right by the missus, for sure."

"T'e flask tingway's gone ... and t'e sachel" Colly butted in with the crash of a drawer.

No longer able to sit at the fire, the three searched the house, and from the various items missing, and a proper recount of her last conversation with Colly, they deducted that Vivian had gone up Mangerton Mountain.

She had spoken to Patrick about it many a time, but he had never been willing to take her. "Shaun, saddle the horses."

"Aye, sir." O'Donaghue slung on some riding breeches and waterproofs. He disappeared out the kitchen door into the wild howling night.

"Colly, if we're not back in an hour, go to the village and tell the sergeant that we've gone up Mangerton Mountain to look for Vivian, and we'll need a search party. Do you understand?"

"To be sure, master Patrick. " the old servant replied "I'll watch tat ol' granfater clock like an old owl, so help me."

Patrick dressed in waterproofs like O'Donaghue. He snapped his fingers and the dogs rose and followed him out the kitchen door to join O'Donaghue in the stable yard.

Colly peered out from the window into the dark, seeing nothing in the rain, only the sound of the masters two fine horses clattering across the cobbles and out onto the road with a thunder of hooves.

*

One of the dogs had found her just above Torc Cascade. Volcano had stumbled on some loose rocks and the cart had gone over the edge of the track throwing Vivian into the gully. Volcano had rolled over on top of her, and certainly would have crushed her to death, had the horse and cart not continued to roll. Volcano had dropped into the raging waters and been swept over the waterfall. It was O'Donaghue who first saw the battered beast lying on the rocks.

Patrick picked Vivian up. There was a gaping wound in her head, the blood had been washed down her face by the rain, but he could see very little in the dark of the night. All he could feel was how cold she was, as if the life had gone from her and all that was left was skin and bone. He thought she was dead, but O'Donaghue, an experienced mountain man, said she was still alive, but had gone into a coma.

"We'll take her down to Torc" Patrick yelled. Neither of them had any idea how long she had been lying out in the rain, perhaps five or six hours, but they both knew that if they had not found her then she would have been dead by morning. Torc House was a half-mile away, and by turn, they carried her off the hills, down on to the main lake road, and burst into the parlour of Torc House, inhabited by Patrick's partner, John Riley.

Riley, a distinguished looking man a few years older than Patrick, leapt out of his chair as if he thought the Tenant's League had come to murder him. When he saw Patrick and Vivian in his arms, he immediately cleared the area in front of the fire, and they laid her on a blanket. They sent O'Donaghue to fetch Doctor MacIntyre while they began to strip Vivian of her drenched garments. Riley went to the linen cupboard to fetch some towels, to the bedroom to collect a nightdress, and finally to the kitchen to bring some brandy. Patrick meanwhile removed the last of his wife's wet things, and then with Riley's help, put her into the nightgown. They put a dressing on her wound as best they could, put a pillow under head, covered her with the blanket, and decided to wait for Doctor MacIntyre.

John Riley had known Patrick twelve years and he had never seen him so distressed. He poured him a brandy and forced him to drink it. Patrick kept staring at Vivian, hoping for the flicker of an eye-lid, the twitch of a finger, anything that might give him hope that she was going to live. He took Patrick in his arms to calm him down, but when he kissed Patrick on the lips,

Patrick threw him off. He pinned Riley against the wall. He was wild with anger. He held his face a few inches from Riley's.

"You bastard! Don't you have any feeling? That's my wife lying there! Are you not ashamed of yourself? Have you no morals? You're disgusting." He held John Riley's shoulders in a vice-like grip. "You care for no one ... only yourself."

Patrick's let go of Riley and crossed the room to lift the limp body of his wife. He rocked her gently. He looked up and saw John Riley standing motionless where he had left him, the flickering flame of an oil lamp casting a menacing shadow across his face.

"All the time's I've slipped away to be with you, all the times I've lived this great lie, listening to your whimpering, telling me I should never have married in the first place. Who the bloody hell do you think you are telling me that you are the only one I have loved." Patrick began shaking uncontrollably, hovering over his wife like a protective animal, eyes motionless, voice trembling. "I never loved you, never. I lied, John, I lied. She's the only one I love. You always wanted it your way, and you had it with me. From your seduction of me at Trinity, the way you wouldn't let me go, the fear of God you put in me, I hated you for it. You schemed to get me to Killarney, to control me, to hide me away from the world to keep me as your lover." Patrick's hold on Vivian tightened "You used me" his eyes closed "You raped me ... I didn't even know what I was doing." He opened his eyes.

"Not any more! It's over. You nearly succeeded in destroying the one decent thing in me, my real love for Vivian. This is who I belong with ... Vivian. There's no place for you!"

"You're upset, Pat ... this is not the time to talk about this." John Riley had been well used to Patrick's outbursts and had always found a way around them before. This time was different.

"No, I won't shut up. You've used me, John; you've ruined my life. Do you think I'm happy thinking about you when I'm with her? You treat me the way I treat her. You criticise everything I do - the way I talk, the way I dress, the servants I keep - I can do nothing right for you, unless I do it your way." He had never felt this angry with John Riley before. He had always been scared to tell him what he really thought in case John had decided he no longer needed him. For Riley, as the senior partner, had become rich and powerful in the county; Patrick was the catholic whipping boy who did all the dirty work, while Riley kept his hands clean by dealing with the court work. It was only now that Patrick finally believed all along what Vivian had said about John Riley - he needed Patrick more than Patrick needed him.

"It's over, John, what we were to one another is in the past. Vivian needs me."

"Have another brandy, Pat." Riley held out the bottle.

Patrick knocked it from his hand and it fell on the floor and smashed. The brandy seeped over the floorboards like blood. "I warn you, John, stay away from me. You lay one more finger on me and I'll kill you. You disgust me. When I think about what I have allowed you to do to me ... You make me sick. Get away!   I don't want you anywhere near my wife!"

With that, Patrick threw himself on the floor with his wife and held her in his arms. He looked into her face and regretted the miserable years they had spent together.

Riley looked on with his cold detached eyes. He could sense that his twelve-year-old relationship with the Ulster boy he had roomed with at Trinity was at an end. In many ways he did not care. Soupers' could never be trusted, they never truly offered up their loyalties the way Protestants did. It was this realisation had recently made him take another young legal man as a lover, a man who did not feel guilty about his homosexual nature. Patrick Trainor could go to hell.

"As soon as the doctor comes " Riley spat "I want you and that bitch out of my house, Trainor, even if it kills her."

Patrick ignored him, and with some anger, Riley went into the kitchen to fetch a cloth to wipe up the spilt brandy. He was meticulously clean and could not stand to see even a picture on the wall that was slightly askew. While he was in the kitchen, O'Donaghue returned with Doctor MacIntyre and Casey, the local police sergeant.

"Casey" Riley said taking him aside "Mr. Trainor wants his wife home as soon as possible. "Get my man Sullivan out of his bed and help him to harness my covered carriage to take Mrs. Trainor home."

Casey did as he was told, for he was in Riley's pocket, receiving gratis payments for 'jobs' beyond normal policing.

MacIntyre dressed Vivian's head wound, and agreed with Riley that it would be best for Vivian to be taken home where she could be tended properly. She was in a coma, and as far as he could guess, it could be days, even weeks before she regained consciousness.

Casey returned to tell them that the carriage was ready. Patrick carried Vivian out, and with MacIntyre's help, placed her in the carriage. They both got into the carriage.

"I'll bring on the horses" said O'Donaghue. "Right, Jack!" he shouted to Sullivan "Lead on!"

Sullivan drove the carriage along the road towards Muckross Abbey and Killarney with O'Donague following on behind with his master's and the doctor's horses.

Riley stood with Casey in the doorway of Torc House. "Soupers, Casey" he said to him out of the side of his mouth "Ungrateful soupers." Casey looked at him with a broad grin. "Come in for a whisky, for there's a bit of Lodge business I have to discuss with you before the next meeting."

*

Vivian recovered consciousness after two days but remained poorly for months. Patrick stayed by her bedside, reading to her, telling her about his childhood, feeding her, running little errands for her, doting on her, kissing her, caressing her cheeks, crying with her about all the unhappy times they'd had, laughing with her about all the silly things they'd argued over or done.

He also told her about his University days, and about Riley, and how he had been sucked into his world and lost his way, and in her own way, she forgave him, forgave him because he was honest with her in a way that he had never been before. For her part she told him about Stephens and the other small matter, and he was neither jealous nor embarrassed, instead he embraced her, and made love to her.

Suddenly, it was as if they were married again, not two strangers sharing a house and leading separate lives; Patrick would lie by her, and they would take each other for comfort, out of love. They talked incessantly, Patrick more than Vivian, for she had contracted pleurisy, an infection of the throat and lungs, and she would convulse with chest pains and cough up fluid, and shiver with cold. It was moments like that Patrick would transfer his body warmth to her, holding her tight around the waist, helping as best he could to ease the pain of her coughing.

As well as he could, he bathed her and helped her keep dignity with the use of a chamber pot, but in these matters she was usually assisted by Colly, a woman with vast experience of illness and the needs of the incapacitated. At times neither of them knew what they would do without Colly and Shaun, for Patrick had neglected almost everything, but his wife. His partnership with Riley had been dissolved, and Riley had taken a new partner, a protestant called Douglas, one of those breeds of British-Irish men with an English mother, a Scottish grandfather, who had been born in India. All the clients that had been so grateful of Patrick's services, switched to using Douglas, and Patrick found that no one required the services of a *souper* lawyer.

It was Vivian who suggested that Patrick went back to being who he was - a catholic Irishman who should be standing up for the rights of his own people. At first Patrick thought it would solve nothing, but he re-entered the catholic faith, and almost overnight, discovered good catholic men and women at his door seeking legal representation.

Patrick had a new fight on his hands - the whole weight of the Irish judicial system that was in the hands of the Trinity Protestants and their English Lord Chief Justice. But he relished the challenge; the road to emancipation was not to become like the masters and change the system from within, but instead, to tear down the system brick by brick, and to rebuild anew.

For the first time, he found Vivian whole-heartedly behind him, and he loved her for it. She became pregnant, and as her health improved, she drew strength from her confinement. As they spent time together in the garden or on short strolls to the loughs, he saw Ireland in all it's glory, not as a part of some mighty empire that ruled the world, but as a country with it's own long history and traditions. He had come to see that the future of Ireland was in it's own making, in his hands, and his children's. All that he would work for in the future would be for them.

Vivian smiled. She had everything she wanted. She gazed up at the old volcano of Mangerton Mountain, and with a little cough, took Patrick's hand and walked slowly back towards the house with the only man she would ever love.

PART TWO

1

The year we re-commence our story is one
of those forgetful years in which the world
at large was at peace. Nothing of great
exception happened in that year to make it
memorable; the French took over Senegal;
Chile seized the northern Atacama from
Bolivia and Peru. People got on with their
lives; the enemy was not some foreign
power or contagious disease; the battle was
one of morals and temperance in the fight
against the capitalist evils of sex, alcohol
and gambling. The people of northern
Europe and eastern America had
succumbed to decadence and become
wicked and sinful and full of temptation. It
was no place to send a young man out into
the world on his own, and even less
thinkable, to allow a young woman to go
anywhere!

Yet, in the face of reality, the era was
heralded as a great age of liberalism,
though the facts were plain for everyone to
see; too much 'do as you please' had
become for many 'take what you want'. The
punishments failed to fit the crime;
murders remained unsolved, crimes went
undetected; vast fortunes were made
illegally; the whole of society seemed to be
pervaded with corruption; people slept
uneasy in their beds; wives suspected their
husbands of adultery; men drank
themselves to death; knocks came on doors

for monies owed; women stood by lampposts under archways; the nights were foggy; the days were wet; the weather in general was awful; everyone felt miserable and depressed.

Not so at the Convent of the Sister of Our Lady in County Meath. The evils of Dublin lay thirty miles away to the south; the brothels; the drinking houses; the con men, the tinkers, the sailors, ready to cheat or rob the innocent and the defenceless. By contrast, everything in the convent was sunshine, wholesome and good. Those who were admitted as patients brought low by vice and circumstance, re-emerged into the world as Sister Goodness or Brother Righteous, women and men cleansed of evil and sin. It was a place of miracles midst a land in turmoil.

This, of course, is completely untrue; nowhere is a complete oasis. It would be mistake to think that twenty-one years in a convent in County Meath had left Lady Elizabeth, known in the convent as 'Sissy' Shum, completely ignorant of the outside world. Throughout her childhood she had been allowed to roam as freely as the other girls at the convent school, permitted to go into Navan on market days; to go on outings to Kells or Tara; to take the train to Laytown to view the sea; she was not shut-off from the world or the world from her. However, she had never been to Dublin; she had heard so many bad things about the capital city, she had no desire to visit it at all.

Sissy, at her coming of age, had an

ordinary appearance and ruddy cheeks from rubbing them too often. Her skin was liberally blighted by freckles, but she had sparkling eyes, good white teeth, a wide forehead, a dimpled chin, and beneath her habit, a full bust. She had an abundance of enthusiasm and energy, but she lacked ambition and drive, and too often, a well-intentioned task was begun, but never completed.

The name of Elizabeth was appropriate for her looks. There are many who will argue that personality is formed by the name given to it, and there are good arguments for this, but even more against it. However, Sissy was a far more appropriate name for the nature of the daughter of Olive Vanya, for she was hot-tempered, warm in her convictions, and inclined to express them freely. She had two close intimate friends in the world - Sister Bonaventure, and her convent school friend Marion.

Sister Bonaventure, the convent name given to Clarissa, was like a mother to Sissy. Clarissa had not told Sissy that she had been her real mother's maid and had travelled to America with her. In fact, Sissy had been told very little about her mother at all. This was not a deliberate ploy by Clarissa or even Sister Gabriella, it was because they thought that knowledge of her breeding and inherited wealth might set her apart from the other children in the convent, most of whom came from poor backgrounds, or like, Marion, were abandoned at birth. Thus, in the interest of fairness and equality, the knowledge was kept from her. They agreed not to tell Sissy anything until the day she reached the age of consent.

*

"Sissy!" one of the younger girls called out into the orchard "Sissy Shum!"

The twelve-year-old girl had been recently orphaned and been in the convent only a few months. She raced up and down between the apple trees searching for the older girls.

Sissy, and her best friend Marion, had finished collecting the apples in baskets. They sat on a stonewall gazing out over the fields. It was a hot morning. They had rolled the sleeves of their whites up around their shoulders and tucked up the hems of their habits to expose their legs to the sun. They stretched back their heads and closed their eyes to catch the rays on their necks and faces.

"This is exquisite, Mari, so it is" declared Sissy in a distinctively Irish accent.

"It's grand it is, for sure" replied Marion "but Sister Bonaventure would kill us if she saw us like this, so she would."

"Bonny's no angel herself. She sneaks off in the late morning for a nap in her cot."

"Now, you learn something every day, so you do" laughed Marion. She was a happy-go-lucky girl of twenty, a couple of months younger than Sissy. She was pretty, tall and slender, with dark eyes and dark hair that the nuns thought foreign. Her eyes were perhaps too round for regular beauty, and her hair would not stay in place; her mouth was large and expressive; her nose finely formed, though some would think it was rather broad. She had, like Sissy, no other life than that of the convent, and had come to accept that one day she would cease to be a lay sister in the classroom, and become a postulant.

Sissy was not so sure. The convent was her home, and she was a deeply religious girl, but there was something that always prevented her from accepting fully the life of a nun. She could not explain it to herself, yet she had always felt that something more was expected from her than from the other children in the convent. Nothing had ever been said, yet, whereas the other children had either left the convent to go out into the world, or like Marion, had stayed to become a lay sister, Sissy had never been asked by the Mother Superior to discuss her future. There was no question that she was the oldest child there. Some of the girls had become postulants at sixteen and gone to do service as missionaries in Africa. At one time, Sissy had thought that she might have liked to do that too, until news reached the convent that Sister Mary Flanagan, a girl Sissy had been very fond of, had died of fever in Sierra Leone, and had been buried in the African earth.

The thought of dying in a far-flung place had sent a shiver of fear down Sissy. One of the other girls had gone to a Woman's College in Dublin, and this too had interested her, until she discovered that the girl had to leave the college before graduation, to give birth to an illegitimate child. The wickedness of the world seemed to be everywhere, and in the words of the Reverend Mother - it is there when you see it, and on you, when you don't.

"Sissy!" called the young girl from amongst the trees.

"Holy Mother!" shouted Sissy and Marion simultaneously, rolling down their sleeves down and throwing down their hems.

"Sissy Shum!" the girl called again "Where are you?" Then, the girl saw the two older girls sitting on the wall. "There you are" she said in an exasperated tone.

"Yes, Maureen McGuiness, here I am" said Sissy mimicking the same tone.

"Can you not be a wee bit quieter" scolded Marion with a straight face. "You'll wake up Sister Bonaventure."

"What?" said Maureen with a vacant look that made her jaw drop and stare open mouthed?

"Shut your mouth, Maureen, or you'll catch flies" joked Sissy. The girl closed her mouth instantly. "Now, stand up straight, and tell me what it is you want me for?"

The girl, faced with the two most senior girls in the convent school, felt awkward and stammered slightly "The Reverend Mother wants to see you in her room at twelve o'clock."

"Yes!!" declared Marion triumphantly, slapping Sissy on the back.

"What do you mean, you eggit? She only wants to see me, nothing else."

"She's going to ask you to become a postulant ... I know it."

Sissy let out a sigh, for at long last, after

years of waiting for something to happen in her life, she was now about to be consulted about her own future.

"What are you going to say to her, then?" Marion asked.

Sissy worshipped Marion. A sense of dread filled her as she saw the look of joy in her friend's face. Sissy wanted to take her vows, to remain at the convent with Marion, where they could spend their mornings and evenings together, just the two of them, intimate and inseparable, but she knew she would be unhappy.

"Oh, Marion." Sissy took Marion into her arms and kissed her on the cheek. "Nothing will come between us orphans."

Marion giggled. "You look like a monkey when you make that face."

"I love you so much, Mari." She threw her arms around Marion and held her tight.

"Are you coming?" asked Maureen impatiently.

Sissy and Marion walked back through the orchard arm in arm, stealing kisses from one another, while Maureen brought up the rear, kicking rotten apples this way or that.

They reached the big door that led along the corridor to the Mother Superior's room. Sissy kissed Marion again.

"I really do love you" she repeated.

"Oh, Sissy, you're a big dope sometimes."

Sissy placed her finger on Marion's lips to prevent her from saying another word. "Wait for me outside the dining hall." Sissy's eyes misted over, then cleared again, as Marion nodded her head, and turned back into the garden.

Sissy followed Maureen through the big door and past the Community Room that depicted the journey of Christ from the judgement to the Cross. The images had always terrified her, but suddenly, with a new understanding, she began to feel inspired by the sacrifice that Jesus had made for the sake of good. Given the chance she would continue the work of God and his Son however she could. It was difficult to imagine how people could live their lives otherwise, to forget that Jesus died for the sins of man, was unforgivable. Jesus was beautiful, so honest, so understanding, he was everything that was perfect. She adored Jesus, she worshipped Jesus, she loved Jesus. She would give her life for Jesus.

By the time Sissy arrived at the door to the Mother Superior's room, she was in a state of euphoria. Whatever the Mother Superior would ask of her, she would do. She had always been obedient to the Mother Superior, looked upon her as the person she would most wish to be like.

She knocked on the door, and entered.

*

Sister Gabriella had never forgotten Olive Vanya. While it is true to say that a wayward woman may come to cherish the simple life of a nun, it is rare to find a religious woman who dreams of being wayward. Of course, this may only be wishful thinking, for there are good documented cases of convent women throwing off the shackles of their faith and sinking to a life of debauchery. Fortunately, however, such cases are rare, and it must be supposed that whenever such thoughts arise in the mind of a truly devout conventual, that the possession of a rosary, and the recall of the seven dolours of Mary, ritually banishes such evil thoughts in a continuous *missa privata*.

Gabriella, now Prioress, had not envied the life of Olive Vanya, but she had admired it for it's independence and tenacity. As a Sister, Gabriella had struggled all her life to do good for people who had fallen by the wayside, fought to defend them against the ill-opinions of society, to clear their names, and return them innocent to the world. As a Reverend Mother, she had abandoned the Samaritan role previously asked of her, and become a dispenser of justice, an arbiter of good and evil, a judge rather than a lawyer. She did not enjoy being a dispenser of justice, but she had been called upon to serve the Lord, and with what influence she had, she tried to help the members of the convent community as best as she was able.

In her heart of hearts, she had always wished that Elizabeth might one day become a postulant and join the religious community proper. Every year, Gabriella had reviewed the development of Sissy, and despite keeping her in the convent three years beyond the normal time for a pupil, she had realised that Sissy would never be happy as a nun. There was too much of the nature of her mother in her, and from what Gabriella had gleaned from

Clarissa over the years, she had also inherited many the traits of her father, Count Rostov.

There was a soft knock on her door before it was opened.

"You wanted to see me, Mother?" Sissy asked

"Sissy, my child, come in."

Gabriella's room was vast, clean, and elegant without ostentation - a bed stood out from the wall, a simple wooden one, and a washstand was concealed in an enormous cupboard. Two large windows opened out into the garden. One of the windows was open - not wide open, but enough to hear anything said in the cloisters below. Close by the window was a little table that Gabriella used as a desk. On it was a fragment of plaster, a representation of the Virgin.

Gabriella took Sissy by the hands and led her to the desk and invited her to sit on a small wooden chair facing the window, while Gabriella, perched herself on the windowsill.

"You're very fond of Marion" smiled Gabriella.

"I love Marion like the Virgin" replied Sissy innocently, almost without thinking.

"But you mustn't love her more than you love God and the Virgin, child. I know it's easier to find quick comfort in companions than in the workings of God, but love of the flesh is the way of sinners."

There was a look of bewilderment in Sissy's eyes. "My love for Marion is a pure innocent love of her spirit, not of the body" she said almost in tears. There had been a case some years before when two sisters had been expelled from the convent when their love of the spirit had turned to worship of the flesh.

"I've watched you in the garden, in the cloisters, in the dining hall .... you constantly touch and embrace one another without reserve. It has been reported that you sometimes share a bed together."

"I'm scared of the dark. You know I've always been scared of the dark. I go to her for comfort."

"You are a grown woman now. There comes a time when childhood passes and adulthood beckons. Perhaps it is my fault that I have kept you too long in the convent."

"But where-else could I go?" Sissy was suddenly frightened. She thought she had been asked to see the Reverend Mother about taking her vows, but the conversation was taking a turn in an unknown direction.

"How many years have you been here, Elizabeth?"

"All my life, Mother. I was born here."

"Yes, Sissy, but how long ago? Do you know?"

"Eighteen years? Nineteen?" Sissy did not know. She had never been good with numbers. Age had never seemed important to her. Birthdays in the convent were never celebrated.

"You are twenty-one next month, my dear, and you will be free to leave the convent."

Sissy looked at Gabriella with a blank expression. What did being twenty-one mean? Why did she have to leave? Gabriella continued.

"I remember the day you were born. Your mother died with you in her arms. We hav'n't told you much about your mother, have we. Or your father?"

"No" said Sissy in a state of shock.

Gabriella called in Sister Bonaventure, and together they proceeded to tell Sissy the story of how her mother came to the convent. It was a long story that took all of two hours to explain, for it covered the years in Vienna as well as Madeira and America, and involved describing how minor connections such as the American consul in Venice, finally led, through the energies of the James's, to her mother tracing her father to Ireland.

All the while, Sissy bit her lip as her mother might have done, not quite believing what she was hearing. She put her elbows on her knees and dug her fists into her cheeks. She was faced with a sense of loneliness, abandonment, and failure, for she knew now why she had never been called to take her vows. Until that moment she had one pair of shoes, one white chemise, a black cloak, and two pairs of cotton socks for all her worldly possessions. Now, she was being told that she was an heiress. The necessity of concealing it from her until then was lost on her, it made everything that had gone before for years appear vain and foolish, like a dream come suddenly to an end. They had not prepared her for the outside world, for it was to the outside world that she now realised that she must go. For a long time she just sat on the chair and gazed at the plaster image of the Virgin. The emptiness of the Mother Superior's desk was nothing to the vast emptiness that had suddenly filled her. She thought about Marion, the apple orchard, market days in Navan. It was the end of things, as she knew them.

Gabriella was an old campaigner in human emotion, but even she on this occasion, sensed that she was scattering her own flock in deference to past events. She had no illusions as to Elizabeth's future, her long experience of spiritual matters, had prepared her for the fatal and unavoidable in the life of the Church. The workings of God presented itself to her most distinctly as a series of calamities overtaking individuals - folly, revenge, and rapacity - part of a divine dispensation. Gabriella's clear-sightedness of this was always served by an uninformed intelligence, but her heart, preserving it's tenderness amongst scenes of shock and despondency, abhorred the present calamity the more the story was unfolded to Sissy.

Clarissa entertained feelings of maternal scorn at Sissy's reaction to the news, for Sissy was clearly unhappy about it, though at the same time, wonderfully angelic. Had she not cared for the child from her infancy? It was the child that had kept her in the convent for more than twenty years. The fresh flowers at the vault of her mother (and father), that was also her doing. Now the time had come to quit the safety of the convent, and rejoin the world, and the child did not want to go. How ungrateful, how unjust!

Whatever the confused state of her feelings towards Sissy, Clarissa repeatedly stopped short to inhale with a strong snuffling noise the scents of the garden, and shook her head profoundly. At the thought of what might become of the new Sissy, and herself, she became gradually overcome with dismay. She voiced it in an agitated murmur.

"Now, girl, pull yourself together." She turned to Gabriella. "What are we going to do, she doesn't want to leave?"

Gabriella pulled one of the fine grey hairs that hung from the line of her jaw, and spoke with a conscious pride in her judgement. "You will go to London."

"London???" cried Sissy

Clarissa, anticipating the day of Sissy's departure, had made up her mind to leave too. The matter had been laid before Gabriella and then examined by the Ecclesiastical Authorities. Through the offices of the Apostolic Delegate, it was dispatched to Rome where it had been carefully examined, and a *rescript* granted. She was to be dispensed from her Vows and the obligations of religious life. She was to be restored to her former condition of secular with complete freedom to return to the world and live there, according to whatever way of life she chose. She knew that wherever Sissy went, she would go with her, watching over her, protecting her from harm, serving her, as she had served Olive Vanya. If it meant going to London, then ......

"I have been communicating with the James's of New England all these years" continued Gabriella. "Myself and Mr. Henry James were two of the trustees of the Rostov estate, but Mr. James died last December, and his daughter Alice, has taken up the trusteeship in his stead. The terms of the legacy are that you are to be seen by the trustees before inheriting your wealth. That would have meant you and myself sailing to America, but Miss James says she is moving to England in a few months to live with her brother Henry in London. We are arranging for all the trustees to meet with you in the offices of *Fletcher & Fletcher* in London. In the meanwhile, some money has been advanced, for your journey to London."

Sissy was upset "I don't want to go to London."

"Sissy, be quiet!" scolded Clarissa "You'll do as you're told. You will not be alone."

"Does that mean that Marion can come?"

"Marion has agreed to become a novice, Sissy" Gabriella replied quickly. "Sister Bonaventure will accompany you. I have given her full proxy to care for you until the meeting of trustees in London. I will join you there later."

"Oh" said Sissy in a tone of acceptance. She did not know what that meant, whether Sister Bonaventure would just journey there for the trustees meeting, or be with her all the time. It was all too much to think about. She burst into tears, and Gabriella closed the window in case the novices in the cloisters heard the young Lady Shum cry.

*

"If I have to leave here, you'll follow me, Mari, you promise" Sissy made Marion swear on the bible.

It would be tedious to attempt relating all, or even one tenth part, of the tender proofs of love and affection which Marion was in daily, let's say hourly, habit of receiving from Sissy once she knew she was leaving the convent. If for only ten minutes she lost sight of Marion, by her walking, or duties, Sissy was in such agonies, that Marion was constantly jibed by the other girls because Sissy ran after her all over the convent. Sissy flatly refused every invitation she received to go with others on visits to Navan, or to the homes of children in the parish, unless Marion was with them, until at last, Reverend Mother Gabriella grew very anger and threatened to inform the trustees about her behaviour.

Sissy would not desist, and her love for Marion grew out of all control. She was sent to confession and received a lecture from Father MacNabb on her connection with Marion, insisting that she leave off her worship for a girl, and return to worshipping the Virgin. The reproach excited Sissy into a spirit of defiance, such as a mild word from the priest never could have produced. She repeated her solemn assurances to Marion that no power on earth could destroy her everlasting attachment, or induce her to leave off seeing her.

Marion deeply regretted that she was not of age, that she might immediately quit the convent, and accompany Sissy to London, if for no other reason than to ease the embarrassment. She reminded Sissy that the period of her coming of age was only two months away and implored her not to irritate the Reverend Mother and Father MacNabb unnecessarily. She did not touch on the subject of them being together forever, but desired her to rest satisfied with her faith, and that she would never willingly cause her a moment's pain while she had reason to believe in her affection. In conclusion, Sissy wrongly concluded that she might expect her in London once she came of age.

On convincing herself of this, Sissy's madness evaporated and calm returned. The two girls embraced, and for the first time in weeks, Sissy went out of the convent with another novice to visit some dying woman in the nearby village.

One week later, on her birthday, Sissy set out with Sister Bonny for London by way of Dublin, Marion seeing her as far as the carriage that collected them at the gates of the convent.

2

In a boarding school in Waterford, fifteen-year-old Patrick Trainor had been cornered by three sixth formers. They had him in their common room and had open a copy of *Tom Brown's Schooldays* at page one hundred and seventy two.

"Now, Trainor, according to the English, we should put you in front of an open fire and toast your backside." Bailey and Donnelly stood on either side of him as Diarmid Wellesley poked him in the belly with his index finger. "But we're Irish, arn't we, and we can put up with a bit of lip when it suits us. Can't we, lads?"

"Certainly, Diarmid" uttered Bailey.

"Aye, we can" replied Donnelly.

"Now, Trainor, we're all gentlemen here. What's a bit of fun between school chums? Shall we break his arms, lads?"

"Feel weak today, Diarmid" declared Bailey.

"Haven't had dinner yet" moaned Donnelly.

"Well, then, Trainor, what will we do with you?" Wellesley asked.

"Come on, Wellesley, it was only a bit of crack. I said I'd seen you doing it with her, but I hadn't really" Patrick pleaded with them.

"I call that slander, Diarmid." Bailey stated emphatically.

"It makes him a little liar, doesn't it" Donnelly suggested.

"Come on, Trainor, what exactly did you see?" Wellesley demanded "or it's the English for you."

Patrick hesitated, then gathered his strength to utter the truth. "I saw you put your thing in her. It was disgusting."

"What was disgusting" laughed Wellesley "My thing or what I did with it?"

"Both!" cried Patrick.

"That's what boys do to girls, you silly idiot," explained Wellesley. "Why else do you think I'd have a girlfriend anyway?"

"If she was your girlfriend, why was Bailey and Donnelly holding her down" replied Patrick. The shock of seeing the three of them doing what they did to a local peasant girl in the hedgerow had fascinated him like nothing else before. He had never seen what girls had under their dresses before. The girl had struggled as Wellesley had forced himself on her. She had cried out, but Wellesley had covered her mouth with his hand.

"He's a little virgin" taunted Bailey.

"Let's get him drunk as a punishment for being a peeping tom" suggested Donnelly.

Wellesley went to a cabinet and brought out a bottle of potcheen. Bailey and Donnelly held Patrick while Wellesley forced open his mouth and poured the whiskey down his throat. He almost choked. Wellesley continued to pour and it ran down Patrick's chin and began to soak into his shirt.

"Stop it! Stop it!"

"Swear as a gentleman you'll tell no one, Trainor, or I'll pour the rest of the bottle down your throat." He forced some more of the vile local drink into Patrick's mouth.

Patrick thought he was going to die. "I swear! I swear!"

"As a gentleman, Trainor" added Bailey wrenching his arm up his back.

"I swear as a gentleman."

"Swear what?" shouted Wellesley.

"I swear I saw nothing."

Bailey and Donnelly let go of Patrick and he fell to the floor in a stupor. The alcohol started to rush to his brain, and the room began to spin.

"Get him to his dorm" snapped Wellesley.

Patrick was dragged to his small fourth form dormitory by Bailey and Donnelly and unceremoniously dumped on his cot. His mind was in spin as the sixth formers abandoned him. He threw up on his bed. Minutes later, he passed out on his bed in a state of fever.

*

Patrick Trainor was expelled and sent back to Killarney in disgrace. His father, Patrick Senior, was outraged that his son had brought shame on the family.

"You imbecile! We send you to the best school in Ireland and you get drunk! What sort of son have I fathered?"

Patrick Snr. had always adored his son. Some would say that he had spoiled him, but how can a father spoil a son if he truly loves him. The boy had received the best of upbringings, wanting for nothing. In return, Patrick had idolised his father, always done what he was told. If there was a fault in the relationship, then, it was that they were never truly open with one another. Patrick Snr. gave his son what he thought he wanted, and Patrick did what he thought his father expected of him. They could talk about fishing, hunting, sport and even politics, but they never discussed emotional matters. Patrick Snr. left such 'small' things for the boy to broach with his mother Vivian.

"I've told you it wasn't my fault, father. Why won't you believe me?" The boy was more than upset. He had been wronged by the three sixth-formers, who after getting him drunk had bribed another boy to inform on him. The headmaster had found him lying in his own vomit and had him removed immediately to hospital to have his stomach pumped. Thereafter he was sent home and his things sent-on after him. He had not been given the opportunity of explaining the situation, and even if he had, he knew he would not be able to tell the headmaster what he had seen the three older boys doing to the peasant girl.

"Your schooldays are over, my boy" Patrick Senior informed his son "We're sending you to your Uncle Tom's in Dublin." Patrick protested, but his father would not listen to him. "You'll work for him, and do whatever he says."

Patrick Senior's brother, Thomas, had done quite well for himself as a wholesaler of clothing. He had worked for his father in the linen factories of Belfast learning the trade, then gone south and set himself up in Dublin selling the factory goods. Over the last ten years he had established a good line of trade with gentry outfitters all across Ireland. He had just opened his own fashionable gents and ladies salons in Dame Street, and the business was going from strength to strength.

Vivian Trainor was ashamed of her only child, but she was willing to forgive him and send him to another school closer to home. Patrick Senior would not consent to it. His mind was made up. Patrick would go to Dublin and begin to make a living by his own labours.

Patrick tried to get his mother to change his father's mind. In the end, he told her the truth about the senior boys, and she in turn told her husband all about it.

"More fool him then for not speaking up!" bellowed Patrick Snr.

"Patrick, have some sympathy for the boy. He promised as a gentleman to keep his word"

"How do we know what the truth is?"

"Don't lose faith in your own son, Patrick!" Vivian was angry. "He's had a horrible experience. He witnessed a rape. He was deliberately poisoned with alcohol. Then, that cruel headmaster sent him to have his stomach pumped as a punishment. Jesus, what sort of permanent damage has it done to him? Boys don't make up stories like this!"

Patrick Senior went to his son's room. He was sobbing. He embraced him and apologised for being so angry with him.

"I will get to the bottom of this, so I will," swore Patrick Senior.

"No, father, I gave my word" cried Patrick.

"You don't hold a man to his word when he has been tortured and wronged. They could have killed you."

The following day, Patrick Senior travelled with his son to Waterford. He contacted the police, and it was confirmed that three men had cruelly attacked a local girl, but that she was too terrified to identify her attackers. Patrick gave a sworn statement that it had been Wellesley, Bailey and Donnelly, and after repeating the story in front of the headmaster, the three were interrogated by the police.

The headmaster asked Patrick Senior for forgiveness, and delivered a particular long and genuine apology to Patrick for his treatment at the school and the hospital.

"And off course, it goes without saying, that you are immediately re-instated to the school." It was an obvious ploy. If the boy could be returned to the school, then perhaps the charges could be dropped and the three seniors quietly expelled rather than prosecuted. The headmaster laid his hand on Patrick's shoulder, but the boy was not moved.

"Well, Patrick, what do you say to Mister Swift?"

"No" said Patrick.

"No?" repeated the headmaster.

"No" said Patrick again "I have decided to go and work for my Uncle in Dublin. He has an excellent business and there are good prospects for me."

Patrick Senior stood by his son's decision. He was proud of him. He had come through the ordeal like a Trainor.

They left the headmaster to his problems, most notably, the Board of Governors inquiry, and went to the most expensive hotel they could find for afternoon tea.

*

The effects of the rape trial lingered on for months. Bailey and Donnelly were acquitted as they were minors, and Wellesley, the only one over eighteen, was given a suspended two-year jail sentence. It had come to light that he was a grandson of the Duke of Wellington, and his defence had been one of 'boys will be boys'. To the conservative wing of the Irish male aristocracy he was a 'good fellow', and they had little sympathy for the little country trollop and the *peeping tom* from Killarney who spoke out against their golden boy. Of Bailey and Donnelly, Patrick never heard of again, but Wellesley was someone who he would cross paths with again.

3

Sissy had to make a lot of adjustments to her life. With the realisation that Sister Bonaventure was once her mother's maid, and that she herself, was entitled to have herself addressed as a Lady (there was some doubt as to whether she had claim to the title of Countess Rostov as her father's lands had been lost and the title bestowed on a distant relative after his death.) However, there was no question that she was a Lady, and the title fixed upon her - Lady Elizabeth Shum of Meath, Lady Shum for short, was a legitimate one. There were no other advantages to the title, no fixed income or civil pension as might be expected in some aristocratic circles; she was in essence, the daughter of a Russian émigré who had lost favour with the Csar's court.

In all respects, Sissy felt herself to be Irish. Ireland was the land of her birth, and Ireland was all she knew. She had been taught Gaelic, learned Irish history by heart, and could cite the long list of Irish High Kings up to the desertion of Tara by Diarmit. She had been told as a child that her parents had not been Irish, but never at any time had she felt, or been made to feel, that she was not pure Irish. She loved Ireland with all her heart, and it had never crossed her mind that she would spend her life anywhere else but in Ireland.

Now, she was not so sure. She had to go to London and await the arrival of a woman from America who would confirm that she was of sound mind and body enough to inherit the monies put in trust for her by her mother. She had discovered through Clarissa that the Sisters of Our Lady had benefited enormously from the money that her mother had left them. Naturally, some of it had gone to Rome, but much of it had been used to re-build the convent school where Sissy herself had been educated. The girls of the school had always been known locally as the *County Coleens*, but it was only now that she discovered from Clarissa that *County* was short for *Countess*, that she became aware that the Countess Rostov had donated the money.

So, with this in mind, it did not then seem so surprising to Sissy that the Reverend Mother had advanced Sissy a sum of money to make the journey to Dublin, and that she had arranged for money to be collected in Dublin for onward travel to London. She had no idea how much money she was due to inherit, nor did Clarissa, for she had never been privy to the financial affairs of the Rostovs, but it shocked them both when they called at the Bank of Ireland at Westmoreland Street and Sissy was presented with one thousand pounds sterling.

"Are you sure there hasn't been a mistake?" asked Sissy "an extra zero put on the end, and that it should be a hundred pounds? That, in itself, is a lot of money."

"Not at all, Lady Shum, it is clearly written in words ... One thousand pounds."

For two women who had been in a convent, one all of her life, it was a fortune. A man was lucky if he managed to earn a pound a month.

Poor Clarissa. Everything in the world had changed almost beyond recognition. The power, speed, noise and general ruthlessness of Dublin overwhelmed her. Her twenty one years behind walls had made that inevitable. She felt like a small and dithering mouse. She was completed dazed.

After her first night in Dublin, Clarissa woke in her unfamiliar surroundings with a new and vague sensation of peace that deepened gradually into one of definite content. It rose from her realisation that what she had believed in when she leapt to freedom was truly worth the loss of her faith. She had no regrets, no anxiety about what lay before her. In fact, she felt like an explorer on the verge of setting out. She was full of spirit of adventure and enthusiasm for whatever might lie ahead, an attitude of mind which seemed to her as surprising as it was fortunate, in view of the trauma of leaving the convent the previous day.

Later that morning, Sissy whizzed her off to a hairdresser, where she superintended the transformation of her shorn locks into a crop. This gave Clarissa more confidence and she began to feel more capable of facing what lay ahead. After that, they set out on a hurricane-shopping raid of all the best shops in Dublin. Shoes. Stockings. Blouses. Lingerie. Hats. It was only the discovery of the shops closing that prevented them from buying more.

4

Patrick had been working in his Uncle Tom's fashion salon for about four months, stocktaking and bookkeeping in the gents half of the salon, when in great surprise, two drably dressed women entered the shop. At first he thought that they must have been lost and that they had entered to ask for directions. The manager, Mr. Wylie, was out for lunch, and the assistant Francis Meachan, a boy only two years older than Patrick, seemed too embarrassed to go forward.

"Can I help you, ladies?" enquired Patrick.

"Yes" replied Clarissa "We are going to London to meet with a famous gentleman novelist, and we wish to buy him an appropriate gift."

Patrick noticed the foreign accent of the Clarissa and studied her with a curiosity that was noted by her.

"Have I said something strange?" asked Clarissa.

"No, not at all, for sure." He had momentarily slipped into speaking with a Kerry brogue. "I just for a moment thought that you weren't from Ireland." He looked at the older woman's companion for the first time. She certainly did not look Irish, her complexion was dark, her eyes were dark blue. She had a bold nose and a pair of full lips that concealed a fine set of white teeth, something rare in an Irish girl. Patrick had long noted that Irish girls tended to have a gap between their front teeth, but this young one, had the straightest and least gaped teeth he had ever seen in his life. She had such liberal freckles and a dimpled chin, he thought she was very pretty. Also, he could not keep his eyes off her breasts pushing through the cloth of her old fashioned clothes.

Clarissa noted the boy staring open mouthed at Sissy.

"Young gentleman" she interrupted his thoughts "can we have some service, please?"

"Certainly, Sister." Patrick went to wave for Francis, but suddenly he changed his mind. He had shown customers around the salon before, and from his stocktaking, he knew exactly where everything was stored. This was the first time that he had known ladies to come into the salon unaccompanied by gentlemen. "Do you have any idea what it is you would like to buy for the gentleman?"

"Certainly not" laughed Clarissa in derision at the suggestion "we've led a very sheltered life." This of course was true for Sissy, but in Clarissa's case, she had been a maid to an aristocratic woman who had accompanied an Empress abroad. She knew exactly what sort of things men cherished, but it was a long time ago, and although she had not completely forgotten, she thought that perhaps men's tastes had changed.

"How old is the gentleman, madam?" asked Patrick in a tone that was polite, rather than prying.

"I couldn't honestly say." Clarissa thought back twenty odd years to Massachusetts and a young Henry James. "Perhaps he is a little over fifty." She exaggerated by ten years, but it seemed safer to think of Mr. James as being over fifty, rather than a shade under forty.

"Well" said Patrick "perhaps half a dozen new neck-ties from our factory in Belfast?"

Patrick, after showing them the range of neckties, proceeded to show them the entire contents of the salon. He instructed Francis to make some tea, and after a bit of fuss, he relented to do so as Patrick was the owner's nephew.

All the while, Sissy was thoroughly amused. She had never been in such a place before, a man's world of suits, hats, gloves, shoes, everything she had seen men wearing, and things she could only imagine them to wear. The men's corsets particularly made her laugh, and Patrick's demonstration of how they were worn, made her break out in a fit of giggles.

Francis arrived just in time with the tea to prevent Clarissa from becoming cross, and the two ladies were feted and seated, and allowed to make their minds up over a cup of Darjeeling.

"We'll take a dozen neck-ties" declared Clarissa "and leave the choice to you."

"Excellent decision, madam." Patrick assumed that the older woman was the girl's mother, for there was striking resemblance. He was very pleased with himself. He had sold twice the amount of ties he had hoped to sell without even mention of cost.

"Could we have them delivered?" asked Clarissa.

"Of course, madam." Patrick suddenly felt deflated. He did not know why, but the excitement of the moment had evaporated. He looked at Sissy, but she looked down with the unmistakable shyness of a nun. He realised it was her that had made him so happy, but now, the purchase had been made, and he would never see her again. "If you give me the address in London, I'll be happy to do so."

"No, no" corrected Sissy, speaking for the first time "deliver them to us at the Dublin Hotel."

Dublin Hotel? Patrick was confused. How could two drably dressed individuals afford to stay in the Dublin Hotel? She gave him a card with the room number. She offered some money.

"No, no, payment on delivery, miss." Patrick stressed. Sissy laughed at her being addressed as 'miss'.

"Now, young man" said Clarissa "can you escort us to the ladies salon."

"Is there a Mrs. Novelist?" enquired Patrick

as he took the Clarissa and Sissy next door to his uncle's fashion salon for ladies.

"Not that we are aware of" replied Clarissa.

"It's for us" said Sissy with a smile. She could see by Patrick's face that he was totally confused. "Bring the neck-ties tomorrow afternoon about four" she whispered so that Clarissa could not hear.

Patrick returned to the gent's salon just as Mr. Wylie was returning from his lunch. It was business as usual, and Patrick spent he rest of the day in the back of the salon picking out the best of the most expensive neck-ties he could find.

*

The garments Clarissa now found herself wearing came as a shock, in particular the undergarments which had the substance of a spider's web. Sissy helped to dress her.

"Here's your foundation garment. Actually, Bonny, most modern girls like their corset tight in case they pop the buttons of their basque."

Clarissa would not wear one, and instead, insisted on wearing long woolly combinations, high-necked and elbow sleeved, decorated with a row of neat pearl buttons down the front, over which a high-necked jersey to below her hips where it met a simple kilted skirt, complete with bustle. What bothered her most were the stockings - white lisle and almost transparent. She refused to wear them. She put on a pair of ample, long-legged white cotton bloomers. Sissy, by contrast, wore everything that was modern including the corset that emphasized her contours, and threw her breasts up in the air like balloons.

"You are not going out looking like that!" declared Clarissa.

"Oh, be quiet, Bonny. You're so old fashioned." She adjusted the corset with expert fingers, until she was satisfied with her cleavage.

Suddenly, Clarissa began to recall the level of living at which Olive Vanya had lived. Their hotel room, after the austerity of her convent cell, was palatial and luxurious. There was a nest of pillows on a down-soft bed between delicately fragrant linen sheets. The room was large and high with tall, wide windows. There were pictures on the walls and mirrors everywhere. The thick pile rug struck a note of rich and satisfying colour. For washing there was a great, deep, blue-veined marble basin, into which hot and cold water cascaded from elegant and highly polished taps. In the convent she had been used to going to bed by the light of a tiny oil-filled lamp like a small glass-ink pot, with a wick that could only be manipulated by a pin. Now she found an amber-shaded gas reading lamp at her bedside. She leaned back at the luxury of her surroundings, and began to think of the future.

Twenty-five years before, one thousand pounds would have been five fold the value it now had, and she had recalled hearing from Gabriella when Olive Vanya had died, that thirty thousand pounds had been left in trust for Sissy. If that was correct, and the money had been banked wisely, then Sissy's inheritance would be in the region of one hundred and fifty thousand pounds!

Clarissa's brain swam just thinking about it. Twenty-one years as a nun had taught her a lot, but it had not helped her any to cope with money matters apart from small amounts for food and toiletries. She began to panic, and confided in Sissy that it was best that Sissy took charge of all money matters as her mother had done, and that she would once again take on the role of maid and housekeeper wherever they resided, helping best she could to get Sissy safely through life.

Sissy cherished Clarissa, who as we know from before, was as much a mother to her as any mother ever was to a child. It had been Clarissa who had nursed Sissy through all her childhood illnesses, and it was to Clarissa that Sissy had always run when in trouble with other children or when having difficulties in class. There had never been a moment in Sissy's life when Clarissa had not been there for her; even that afternoon on which Clarissa had slipped on ice and broken her arm while Sissy was on her back, Clarissa had come and kissed little Sissy goodnight in her bed. It had always been Clarissa who had taken her to market in Navan or the seaside, or some ancient monument perched on some windswept hill, for Clarissa had a love of travelling, even if it was only an exploration down a country lane, or a short train ride on a new piece of track. By all accounts, to outsiders free of the confines of convent life, such a relationship would have required Sissy to address Clarissa as 'mama' and not by the formal name of Sister Bonaventure, the name given to her by the Sisters of Our Lady.

"I am no longer Sister Bonaventure, Sissy. I have not used my own name for so long now that it sounds even strange to me. But from now on, you must call me Clarissa as your mother did. Will you do that?"

The name sounded strange to Sissy, for she had known her as Bonny for all of her life. "Clarissa ... Clarissa ... " Sissy repeated over and over again. "I can't call you that. You will always be Bonny to me. My Bonny, my own dear Bonny." Sissy threw her arms around Clarissa's neck.

"Oh, Sissy, you big child" she whispered in her ear and stroking her hair. "Whatever will we do with you?"

"Don't ever leave me, Bonny. Do you promise? Please, promise." Sissy pleaded.

"I'll never leave you, liebling, never...."

*

Dublin in the afternoon, with the sun shining, was a city of gaiety. The redbrick Georgian mansions with their fine doors, fanlights, and little iron balconies outside the first floor-windows, stood back neatly from the wide roads, quiet and dignified.

Patrick had ties neatly wrapped in a box under his arm. He had thought of taking an outside car to the hotel, but the weather was so fine, and the hotel not so far away, that he decided, without Mr. Wylie's knowledge, to walk.

He wondered why Dublin had always been referred to as *Dear Dirty Dublin.* Admittedly, the roads outside Dublin were dirty, but the city itself was like a new penny. The Wicklow Hills stood clear-cut against the sky, from which on a clear day, a man could see the mountains of Wales. Patrick thought that a day like today was just the sort of day a man could see the Welsh mountains, but he could not be certain, and would not believe anyone-else until he had seen them for himself.

In his first months in Dublin, Patrick had been lost in the maze of Dublin streets, and had not liked the Dublin 'accent', but he had very quickly come to know his way around the city, and even come to like Dubliner's intonation and the habit of giving a little upward kick to the end of a sentence. He found himself imitating them, for there were many Dubliners who when they heard Patrick speak, mocked him like an idiot because of the lilting Kerry speech he had learned from his mother, which he could not hide, despite almost four years at boarding school. Patrick was proud of his Kerry upbringing, but it did seem easier to take on the speech of Dubliners than to be jibed by them.

The crowds in the Dublin streets were vastly different from Killarney crowds on market day. They had a haggard money look which he would discover later in life was characteristic of all large cities. There was less laughter. There was painful rushing about. There was a cheerless edge to Dublin, a formal bad temper, which made it easy to realise that the city was passing through dark times. There was a lot of resistance and resentment to Home Rule in Dublin despite the efforts of the Fenians and nationalists like Parnell campaigning in the city. There were certain superficialities that had significantly convinced Patrick that Dublin was a British city, and not an Irish one. The Irish green had vanished from the streets; the pillar-boxes were red; so were the mail vans. The street names were written in English and there was not a word of Gaelic to be seen anywhere. Most of all, statues of Queen Victoria, George IV, and other English monarchs appeared to be in every square; streets were named after English lords, and Union flags fluttered from every state building. His father and mother were heavily involved in nationalist politics, but at fifteen, he had better things to do with his time than worry about bald men arguing with one another.

As Patrick entered the hotel, the lower rooms were a sea of afternoon teas. Men in riding breeches and girls in habits with mud on their boots and wind in their cheeks, stood idly gossiping about the day's events. They had been out hunting with the Meath or Kildare Hounds and had got back to Dublin in time for tea. The nearness to the country and to horses was an abiding passion of the aristocracy, but Patrick had no time for it. In Kerry he had taken enough riding as a boy, and now saw no reason to mount a horse unless it was to visit someone. To gallivant about the countryside causing mayhem with peasants' crops and farmers livestock was not his idea of good sport. He did not like shooting grouse or stalking deer either, he preferred to grass trout. Fishing had been his first love since he had been shown how to fly rod when he was eight by old O'Donaghue.

Patrick knocked gently on the door of a room on the first floor. It opened.

"Yes" a pretty young woman asked as he stood there with the box of ties resting in his arms.

"Oh, sorry, miss" he stammered "I 'tink I've got the wrong room." He swore at himself for dropping his pronunciation on the word think.

"No, no, you have the right room" replied the girl stepping out into the corridor and closing the door of the room behind her.

"It's you!" uttered Patrick in complete surprise, suddenly recognising Sissy as the girl who the previous day had been dressed in dull, uninspiring attire. He looked her up and down and could not believe what he was seeing.

Sissy was dressed in a tight fitting bodice and a loose bustled skirt that showed a hint of ankle. It was all the fashion in Dublin, and Patrick had seen many of the wealthy girls leaving his uncle's salon dressed in such clothes. She twirled on the toes of her calfskin bootlets, swirling her skirt to the height of her upper calves.

"Do you like it?" she asked as she came to a halt with her hands on her hips. Patrick was dumb-struck. How could this be the same girl? He scratched his head. "Don't you like it?" she asked again with a look of hurt

"It's wonderful" said Patrick. Sissy's face lit up like a young child's. "You got your clothes from my Uncle's shop, didn't you?"

"Your Uncle?" quizzed Sissy. She had no idea that the young shop assistant was anything other than a shop assistant. She had wanted to have his opinion of her taste in clothes before she went out into the world. She had heard that London was very fierce, and that people, in particular women, were very critical about what young ladies wore.

"He's very rich" continued Patrick. This was fairly true. Patrick lived with his Uncle and Aunt in a very grand Dublin house. "He has ten servants, at home, we only have six." This was also true. Patrick Senior and Vivian had taken on a larger house than before, some would call it a castle, and it had required the employment of three extra servants in the house, and one extra to help O'Donaghue look after the grounds.

"Would you like to take tea with me?" asked Sissy. There was something about the young man that she liked, and it was obvious that he had good manners and would know how to order tea without it being an embarrassment. After all, these things were all new to Sissy, and she felt that she needed to learn some of the ways of a lady before they sailed from Kingstown for Liverpool, then by train to London.

"What about your mother?" asked Patrick "Won't she mind?"

"My mother! That's Bonny, my maid" she replied curtly "And no, she won't mind,

she's having her afternoon nap, that's why
I asked you to call at four."

Patrick was surprised by the honesty of the
last remark. So she had planned for his
arrival, deliberately engineered him to
arrive at precisely four o'clock while her
maid was sleeping? Suddenly, he panicked.
What if she found out he was only fifteen?
She looked all of twenty, and surely she
would laugh at him and treat him like a
baby if she discovered his true age. He
began to fumble the box of ties.

"What will I do with these?" he asked.

"Bring them with you. I can look at them
while we're having tea." Sissy was firmly in
control of the situation, and Patrick,
knowing that it was best to do as he was
told, shrugged his shoulders and followed
her along the hotel lobby to the stairway
that led downstairs to the foyer.

"What sort of tea do you recommend" she
asked him as they descended.

"Well" said Patrick, for he knew a lot about
teas because his mother had stocked every
type of tea under the sun in the kitchen
pantry. "On a day like this I quite like a
black Assam, without milk, but that might
not be to your liking as it is very strong, as
are some of the Ceylonese varieties that
Lipton's import, but I would say............."

They went into tea and did not stop talking
until after ten o'clock that night when
Patrick left the hotel, saying he would ask
his Uncle for the following day off work so
that he could show Lady Elizabeth the
sights of Dublin.

*

It was ambitious of her to think that anything would come of her friendship of Patrick, he was after all, only eighteen, and she was a full three years older. On top of that, she had sworn herself to Marion, though on reflection, now that the convent had been left behind, she had begun to doubt if she could stay constant in her emotions. She adored Marion, but it seemed much more natural to be with a boy like Patrick than her dear childhood friend. All during her day with him, she wanted to throw her arms around him the way she did with Marion, joke with him, play foolish games with him, but all the while she was reminded by his calling her 'Lady Shum' that she was not expected to be like that. When, finally, she got him to be less formal and call her Elizabeth, he used the name as a substitute for 'Lady', stiffly and formally, as if calling her by it was an honour. It made her laugh. For to be a convent girl one day, and a lady the next, was the strangest experience, and after some hours, she came close to letting it slip to Patrick while they were gazing at the pages of the Book of Kells in Trinity College.

"It's a work of genius" he was telling her. "The monk who painted the pages of this book was a Leonardo da Vinci."

"Surely you mean Michelangelo?" corrected Sissy. She felt that she knew these things. "We studied the Book of Kells at the convent." The Book of Kells was a book of the Gospels illustrated by an unknown monk in Kells monastery in the seventh or eighth century. It had been long wondered how a man could pen such microscopic designs in perfect sections no larger than a postage stamp which had no flaw without the use of a magnifying glass, for they had not been known in those days. Sissy and her fellow pupils had spent hours and hours of their education copying the interlocking lines and spirals.

Patrick was quick on the uptake.

"You went to a convent school?" he asked, surprised she was a catholic like himself.

It was then that she told him everything. It took a three mile walk, first across the Liffey, then back again, a visit to see the mummies in St. Michan's, and finally to pray in Christ Church Cathedral at the statue of the orphan with the stone tear, before she was finished.

"You mean, you never knew your mother or father?" Patrick thought the whole story incredulous. His parents were so boring by comparison.

"Do you think it will change me?" she asked him earnestly.

"I say, it will. One hundred and fifty thousand pounds???" Patrick could hardly get his tongue around the words because the figures were so large.

"It's only a guess. It might be less." She was trying to sound a little less rich so as not to entice Patrick. She could see how the mention of money made his eyes twinkle like gas lamps.

"Well, you better marry me" he exclaimed, throwing his hands up in the air. He did it in such a way that Sissy did not feel the least embarrassed.

"I'll be telling your mother about what you said, Patrick Trainor" she answered quickly. It was something she had heard the Navan girls say to the boys at market days and it had always made everyone laugh.

Patrick did not laugh. He visibly winced. The thought of his mother hearing that he had asked a twenty-one year old to marry him worried him no end. "Don't joke with me, Elizabeth" he blurted. "You don't take me seriously at all, do you?"

"Oh, Pat" she said, taking him by the hand. She wanted to say that he was just like a big baby, but she did the kind thing, and told him something that would make him want to kiss her. "You're the kindest man I've ever met." She had never met any men (anyway, not the sort of men she would consider her equal), so there was some truth in her statement.

It was growing dark and the lamplighters were passing along the narrow lane of Temple Bar. Sissy pulled Patrick into the shadows and kissed him. Despite what everyone thought about her, she had been quietly kissing village boys since she was thirteen. In the summer they were always hanging around the convent grounds, and over the years she had gone into the woods with a number of them. She'd had her breasts squeezed and her vagina explored, not without her discovering that boys had testicles and penises. The variety of them interested her, but she had never allowed any of them to enter her. She was not silly, she had learned enough in the convent from the gossip of the older girls to realise what happened if a boy got inside you with his worm. The worms did not frighten her, it was what the Reverend Mother would say when the baby arrived nine months later. That's why it had been much safer being fondled by Marion than a boy, for she knew that Marion's fingers, or the safe use of a candle, had no damming outcome.

Patrick had never been kissed before at all, except by his mother, Colly, and his auntie Edna, the wife of his uncle Tom. As Sissy's wet lips descended on his own, his oral juices began to seep out the edges of his mouth until he had soaked both their chins with saliva.

Sissy pulled back and ran the back of her hand across her lips. "You're an awful kisser, Patrick Trainor, so you are."

"I'm out of practice since coming to Dublin" he said quickly placing his hands on her breasts that looked as though they were about to pop the buttons of her bodice. Sissy responded by running her hand down the buttons of his trousers, popping them open, plunging her fingers into his pubic hairs, taking hold of his penis with her thumb and forefinger and tickling and gently squeezing his testicles with her other fingers. Patrick drew her lips to his neck as she slid her hand further between his legs and pushed her index finger into his anus. She was hurting him, but the sensation was so extraordinary, he lessened the pain and increased the pleasure by stretching up on the ends of his toes. With is own hands he pulled up Sissy's long skirt until his hands felt the flesh of her arse, and with a heave, he lifted her off the ground until her finger slipped out of his anus and she has high enough to wrap her legs around his waist. She plunged her mouth on to his, pushing her tongue deep into the back of his throat, while he thrust his fingers past the constraints of her underwear and plunged them into her hairy crevasse. He felt the folds of her pussy give way, and in an endless rush, the tips of his fore and index fingers slipped up her hot vagina, and as she wriggled her tongue inside his head, his fingers slid up her to his knuckles. He began to feel fluid drenching his fingers as Sissy reached down and took hold of his cock and pulled its foreskin backwards and forwards. The violence of the movement hurt him immensely, but involuntary, within moments, he stiffened as a great wave of pleasure rose and he ejaculated in her hand.

Sissy felt some sticky substance squirt on to her bum, quickly cool, and run between her buttocks. She removed her tongue from Patrick's mouth.

"How d'you feel?" she asked him with smile. She could hardly see him in the dark, but she could hear his deep breathing and feel the sweat on his brow. She ran her lips across his forehead, then gave him a gentle kiss on the bridge of his nose.

"O'i feel grand" he replied in Kerry dialect. He searched for her lips, all the while, easing his fingers out of her vagina.

"What's happening?" she enquired in a

whisper.

"What do ye mean?" asked Patrick in surprise.

"I haven't had my *bang* yet."

"You mean, you want me to put it in?" he suggested. He knew that it would not be possible to get it hard for another few minutes at least.

"No, you eggit. Women have *bangs* as well. Don't you know that." Patrick did not have a clue what it was he was supposed to do next. Sissy kissed him again. "Never mind" she said to him in a caring tone.

Sissy had become very used to masturbating. One of the older girls had shown Elizabeth how to do it when she was twelve. In turn she had shown Marion, and they had practiced on one another. It had been Sissy's idea to try licking, and it had seemed strange and tickled at first, but they had got used to it, and finally managed to bring one another off by licking and sucking. The Sisters had never caught them, and they had played with one another as a sort of game, competing with one another to see who could get the most *bangs* in a week. Eventually, when they reached the age of sixteen, it had become embarrassing to talk about it, and only occasionally would they sneak off together to the orchard or the fields to bring each other off. By then Sissy had become interested in boys. Marion had never shown the same interest in boys as Sissy, and had often seemed jealous when Sissy had gone off into the woods with one. They even argued about it, but Mari had always been too much in love with Sissy to argue for long, so that Sissy knew she could do as she pleased.

Sissy lowered her legs from Patrick's waist until her feet touched the stone flags of the doorway in which they had stolen their minutes of passion. She opened her purse and took out a handkerchief. She wiped her hand on the hanky, then reached under her skirt and placed it between her legs. "I'm very wet" she giggled. She pushed her skirt back down over her long legs. "Will you take me back to the hotel now, buoyo?" she asked with a peck on the cheek.

Patrick finished buttoning his flies. He looked up and down the lane, then with Sissy on his arm, led her out into the evening hustle and bustle of Wellington Quay, and guided her along the banks of the Liffey pointing out barques and brigantines smelling of salt and sea.

*

The departure from Kingstown was one of those departures that Clarissa had made so many times with Sissy's mother. On the quay was the shop boy, throwing his arms in the air waving goodbye, and shouting out "God be with you!" and "Don't forget to write!" and a dozen other of the last minute exclamations that young people make before and just after the gangplank is withdrawn and the hawsers are cast off. For youth is blind to separation and lost, it steadfastly behaves as if partings are forever, that they are not temporary, while vainly concealing a belief that some day in the near future, loved ones parted from, will be reunited with. In middle age, partings have the appearance of being only for a short while, not forever, while deep inside, the individual knows that the chances of being reunited are a chance in a million.

Yet, as we have already witnessed, millions had left Ireland a generation before, and a further million had left during Clarissa's twenty two year stay there, never to return. Clarissa had arrived with Olive Vanya, and was now departing with Olive Vanya's daughter. To Clarissa, life seemed to have continuity, but that continuity was the Shum family, nothing else. Deep down she still felt herself to be Viennese, but as the shores of Ireland slipped into the wake of the ship, she knew she had also become part Irish. She had spent half of her forty-four years there, almost her entire adulthood, but she was happy to be moving on. She knew she would never return to live in Ireland. There now seemed no need to lay flowers by the tomb of Olive and Grigori, her twenty-one years of devotion and clinging to the past were over. There was now a future, a bright enormous future as the companion of Sissy, an intelligent, articulate, and wonderful girl who had all the qualities of her mother, but none of the coquettishness or hatred of men that so marred her mother's happiness.

Sissy, by contrast, was still thinking about her time in Dublin, in particular, her time with Patrick. He made her laugh, and had been so easy to talk to, she felt that after their afternoon tea and their day together seeing Dublin, that she had known him all her life. She wanted to speak to Clarissa about her feelings for Patrick, to ask her if it was normal to feel affection towards a boy without knowing him for years, but she knew she would not approve of it. Instead, she made do by saying to Clarissa that she had enjoyed her outings with Patrick, and that if he were to come to London, she would return his kindness by taking him on a tour of the city.

This pleased Clarissa, for she felt it important that a girl like Sissy made friends wherever she went. Friendship was what made life bearable. Clarissa had cherished the friendship of Gabriella; she had been the first and only true friend that Clarissa had ever made. Olive Vanya had never really made other friends beside the Empress Elizabeth. Clarissa had often felt that if Olive had remained in Vienna, then some cure would have been found for her illness, for Vienna was awash with the finest physicians in Europe, despite the claims of the Scotch doctors practising in Ireland that they were *au fait* with the latest treatments and medicines. In her opinion, Viennese doctors would not have let her die. This, of course, was no slight upon Gabriella, who without doubt, had kept Olive Vanya alive long enough to give birth to Sissy. Gabriella had done all she could for her mistress, and afterwards, helped Clarissa to integrate into the convent community. It was Gabriella who had taught Clarissa English (even if it was with a Meath accent), and it was Gabriella who had saved Clarissa from a nervous breakdown.

We shall not go into that here, for the manner in which Clarissa descended into a state of nervous exhaustion after the death of Olive Vanya is not a happy tale, for it took almost three years to bring her back to a fit state in which she could cope with the world. There had always been worries that one day she might lapse into the same withdrawn and uncommunicative state which had left her catatonic for so long, motionless, rocking to and fro for hours on end.

As already stated, we shall not go into the details further than to say that nineteen peaceful years had passed since then; years in which Clarissa had given up any desire for marriage, or even a child of her own. She had Sissy, and as a spinster nearing forty-five, having recently renounced her vows, she intended to lead a quiet life, visiting churches and cathedrals, looking in on orphanages, behaving charitably and fairly with all those she met. If she had one ambition, it was to visit St. Peter's in Rome, to hear the Pope. That, above all, would make her content for the rest of her life, that, and a secure future for her adopted child, Sissy.

5

Edward, Prince of Wales had a gay and luxurious life that suited his temperament. He relished his role as an elegant fashion statement although it required him to change his clothes six times a day. His allowance was a one hundred thousand pounds a year, but he could not make ends meet. His extravagances were were so great he was forced to spend part of the year visiting the shire homes of aristocrats, bankers and businessmen who could house and entertain him and his entourage.

Unlike his mother, Edward dispensed with prudery and propriety. He was happy to dissipate the wealth accumulated by his forefathers. As a gentleman, he followed in the footsteps of George IV, and concentrated on the pursuit of pleasure. He was a young blood who preferred to ignore the industrial revolution. Hunting, horse racing, and pretty women were his loves; his greatest enemy was boredom and his own company.

Edward was the leader of the heavy swells, and his favourite activity was to make alliances with *demi-mondaines,* fashionable attractive women who were ready to make themselves agreeable to him if he satisfied their expensive tastes. He furnished his 'soiled doves' with pleasant love nests where he could enjoy their favours.

The reality of the situation was that his mother's frequent absences to Balmoral had left the burden of state duties on his shoulders and he had become weary of it. He was in no hurry to be king. He continued to throw parties with his pal Thomas Lipton, the Glasgow greengrocer turned millionaire, and to be seen with consorts such as Lillie Langtry.

Victoria, in the manner of the grand Empress, frightened that Edward was going to kill himself by contracting syphilis, had banned him from reading the minutes of cabinet meetings. She was always thinking about who was going to succeed her. Edward was disgracing her, and she'd happily pass him over in favour of George, Edward's son. Parliament was also concerned about the monarchy as the Queen's absence from public duties had fuelled republican sentiment. With Gladstone pushing for home rule for the Irish, Queen Victoria saw the need to prop up the Empire at home, not in Africa or Asia.

"To hell with the old bitch!" Edward declared to Lipton while looking along the barrel of his gun "She's up at Balmoral fornicating with that gillie Brown. She's like a stray on heat whenever she's near him." He let fly with both shotgun cartridges.

"Ah woudnae say anything against the Queen, Eddie" replied Thomas Lipton "or anything for her." He let off his rounds, and a bird dropped.

Edward laughed and slapped his old friend on the back. Tom was one of the few people in the whole country who understood him.

"When's the Empress Elizabeth coming back again?" the tea-magnate asked out of curiosity, for Lipton was as much a womaniser as the Prince of Wales.

"You'll have no chance with her, Tom. If you can't ride, you'll not ride her."

They both howled with laughter and went

arm in arm from their hide. They went down through the Norfolk heath towards the beaters and the dogs gathering at the foot of the hill. It had been a poor day's shooting, but neither of them cared.

6

Henry James was enjoying his return to London. He was trying to make good his proposal to his Boston publisher to write a novel about half the length of his successful *Portrait of a Lady*. It was to be a book about the emancipation of women, giving her the vote, releasing her from bondage, co-educating her with men. His father's crusade had been the emancipation of black slaves, but for Henry Junior's generation, the great question of the day was the freedom of women. He would write The Bostonians as a tribute to his father whose death he was still mourning, he would bring to life his father's preoccupations by dramatising them through themes and characters. It would be his masterpiece.

He had set to work at his writing desk, but nothing of The Bostonians had appeared on paper. Everything he began ended as a short story. Today was already tomorrow, and tomorrow next month. At the age of forty, he felt that he deserved something better than rented rooms. There was, after all, something to the adage that life began at forty. He was no longer content to slum it as he had done before, he wanted more from life, a house or a large flat where he could entertain comfortably. He could not wake up day after day and face the idea that he was still poor. Everything about his surroundings reduced him to weakness. If it were not for the distraction of his writings, or the numerous friends he visited or visited him daily, then his rented rooms in Bolton Street would have driven him to despair. He looked at a house in St. John's Wood, but decided against it as it was too far from the centre of things. It came as a surprise, when he returned from St. John's Wood to Bolton Street, to find that his rented flat was rather quite attractive, and with so much writing to do, the thought of moving scared him even more than the thought of staying. He surveyed his rooms and decided that they would do for the present.

Henry had no desire to marry. He was of limited income, and knew that he would never marry, as he was both happy enough and miserable enough without upsetting the balance. He had convinced himself that singleness fitted much better with his view of existence and his lack of interest in having children of his own. A smiling Mrs. James was not one of the articles of furniture he wished to put in his new house when he got one.

He received a steady flow of letters from America, mostly replies to the letters he himself had sent. William Howells regularly corresponded with him, for he had been in London the previous summer, and Henry had helped the Howell family move into lodgings in South Kensington. Howell's had spent the previous fifteen years as editor of the literary magazine Atlantic, a soul destroying job after his interesting and romantic posting as American Consul in Venice. He had married his childhood sweetheart, spawned a family, and led a life of enforced bondage.

Henry and Bill Howells had taken long strolls together.

"Ya know, Henry" Howells said strongly "we're old potbellies now, but when I walk with you, I feel as though we're young again. Just for an instant, I felt as if we were back in Newport twenty five years ago."

They talked about their past, for the future seemed to stand still when they were together. On one occasion they talked about Countess Rostov.

"I suppose if Willy and I hadn't run into the Count in Paris, she'd never have gone to Ireland." Henry could still see the scarred face of the blind count vividly.

"I meant to ask you, Henry ... is Isabel Archer in *The Portrait* based on Olive, Henry?" Howells weakness seemed to be his inability to look beyond what his eyes had seen. He was a second or even third-rate talent who would always be a small writer. He had no gasping imagination, and his job as editor of The Atlantic had starved him into invisibility.

"I mean, Henry, Olive Vanya's drive towards self-annihilation, the fact that she was an orphan, and the absence of parents, the travelling .... it's all a bit too close to be coincidental."

Henry had often wished that he had been

an orphan, to escape the control of his father. He had explored this theme in *The Portrait*. Bill Howells could not see that characters in novels were as fictional as the novel itself.

"Perhaps some of the other characters you can see through, Bill, recognise them as skeletons of my father or sister or some other friend, but Isabel is a dream, a complete fabrication, what might be if women remained liberated and did not shackle themselves to men. That is the undoing of truly great women, and conversely, of all men. Mary, Queen of Scots had everything going for her until she married Darnley. Would Catherine the Great have been great if she'd married? Or Elizabeth of England?"

Bill Howells sensed that Henry was on his high horse.

"If you'd met Olive Vanya" Howells continued "as I met her in Madeira, and later in Venice, you'd understand that Isabel Archers do exist, and that no man on earth can chain such individuals. I say the difference between your fictional Isabel and Olive Vanya is, that Olive Vanya didn't have a self-destructive streak. She wasn't flawed in that sense ... she'd have died had she had the baby or not. She told me in Venice her mother died of an illness that'd been passed down in her family for generations and that she didn't expect to live to old age. She'd only one regret in life ... that she'd not had a child from Count Rostov. He besotted her. She couldn't explain why, but she couldn't get him out of her head. All my time with her, she spoke little about herself, always about the Count, and the Empress, an even more depressing subject than the Count. It seemed to me that she was living her life for other people, that the real Olive Vanya had gone from her entirely. She was easily bored, and when we were together, there were long periods of silence during which she'd sit and stare at some distant point without recognition of anything about her. Eventually I coaxed the admission that at times like those she thought only of the Count Rostov and that life seemed completely pointless without him. I never discovered how he'd managed to capture her mind so completely, for she's still the most beautiful woman I've ever met. When I look at my wife Sally, I wonder how my life might have turned out if I had not run to catch that boat in Madeira, which took me away from her the first time. And again, when she came to my office out of the blue and asked to go to America, had we not argued about some guitar-playing gypsy girl, we might've picked up where we left off and become lovers. I did go to bed with her one afternoon in the heat of the day, but we just caressed, we never fully undressed, we never quite consummated our friendship. I always regret that, for as the years go by, time and time I feel that I've failed in love. I re-live that afternoon over and over again, our conversation, and how I held back telling her that I loved her."

Henry looked at his old friend with some pity.

"There, Bill, you're like Isabel Archer, you've set yourself on a course of self-destruction. You're torturing yourself and you love it. See. that's what is wrong with most people, they wallow in misery and doom. You displease other people and you can't handle it. You like to be thought well of all the time, and so you self-destruct rather than telling Sally 'I don't love you. I've always loved somebody else.' ..... Hell, you punk, don't you think she's been able to see that for the last twenty odd years? Who're you kidding pal? Not me, not Sally. She's talked to me about it, and she's just happy you've found somebody to love, even if she's dead. All she's ever wanted is a father for her four kids. She thinks love's for the birds."

Bill Howells sulked for a moment. They carried on walking, and a short while later, he broke the silence. "Won't you ever marry Henry?"

"Not if she were even a millionairess" replied Henry.

At the end of the summer, William Howells had returned with his family to Loiusburg Square, Boston, pursuing his own career as a novelist, writing to Henry from time to time, to tell him about his sister who lived close by.

*

Alice James was a lesbian. She had befriended Katherine Loring and spent her entire life in Boston. They had been friends for ten years, but everyone knew them to be lovers. It had often been remarked that

Alice was not like other women, but it was Loring who had the brute superiority of a man, to the extent that she was capable of using a rifle. She had saved Alice from a suicidal breakdown.

Alice and Katherine spent all their time together, but they lived in separate apartments, partly because Katherine wanted it that way. When Katherine sailed with her father and sick sister Louise for England, in the hope of finding a cure for her sister's tubercular condition, Alice pined for months until Katherine returned to help her to pack and join her permanently in England.

Alice was to be met by Henry at Liverpool. She had never understood why her father had made her a trustee of the Rostov fortune rather than William or Henry. Katherine had asked her about the Rostov child, but Alice had been unable to fill in the slightest detail bar what she remembered of Olive when she was a child, and that was not very much. Nor did she know how much the fortune was worth, for the money was invested in London, and she had not bothered herself to find out. She had no interest in the Rostov's whatsoever, and the task of assessing the girl's competence to inherit the fortune seemed to her to be a very silly idea. She remembered that her brother William had said that the Count Rostov had died mad, so she assumed that it was the Count who had come up with the silly terms put upon the inheritance of the fortune.

This was not the case. It had been Olive

Vanya who had set the conditions. She had not wanted her child to inherit Grigori's money without having a few competent adults to watch over him (for she had assumed it would be a boy). She had seen how riches had spoiled Ferdinand Maximillan, Franz Josef's brother, and she had not wanted that for her child. Gabriella and Henry Senior had been two of her best choices, but she had not planned for the death of Henry Senior and the transfer of the trusteeship to Alice. Even at the age of twelve, Olive had seen Alice to be a crisis of nerves, prone to illness, physical and mental, alert but at the same time irrational, critical and intolerable.

Alice knew she always had Henry to fall back on. Katherine could not be with her all the time. So as she left Boston, ill and exhausted from worry, she knew she could count on her brother no matter what.

*

Sissy and Clarissa arrived in London safely and settled into a room at the Savoy Hotel in The Strand. It was their plan to visit Henry James in Bolton Street the following morning, but Mr. James sent word that he was going to Liverpool in the morning and that he would prefer to call that evening and take Lady Elizabeth for dinner.

"What shall I wear, Bonny? Red or black?" She held up two evening gowns.

Clarissa had not been asked such a question for over twenty years. "Well" she pondered, "your mother would have chosen the black one, I think."

"Then it's red for me!" Sissy stated conceitedly. She had always wanted to wear red, but it had not been permitted in the convent. "Do you have Mr. James's ties, Bonny?" In the space of a week, Sissy had learned more and more to treat Clarissa as her servant. Clarissa accepted her new role, in fact encouraged it, for it was her intention to serve Sissy as she had served her mother. Sissy, for her part, was enjoying her new status as Lady Shum. "Now, when he comes, Bonny, I will insist that you chaperone me. You know what awful stories about men and young ladies in London. I don't want to end up as a curiosity in Madam Tussaud's" She joked in an off-hand manner that hid her excitement at having dinner with an unknown man. She had read The Portrait of a Lady during the train journey from Liverpool to London, and it had affected her deeply. Henry James had to be a genius! How could a man be so understanding of woman? She had to meet him! Clarissa, of course, would not be allowed to eat with them; she had made her mind up about that. She would be obliged to wait for them somewhere nearby, and at exactly ten o'clock, come to tell her that it was time to go home. Sissy would rise and graciously decline Mr. James's offer of escorting her back to the hotel, he would insist, she would give way, and on the journey back, allow him to propose seeing her again.

It was a young girl's dream, for when Henry James arrived, and introduced himself in the hotel lobby, she immediately perceived that he was over-weight; that his profusion of hair was on his chin and not his bald head; that he was a chain smoker who smelled of mothballs; and that his eyes drooped and his wrists hung limply like a woman's. In fact everything about Henry James seemed to droop; the ash on his cigarettes; the seat of his crumpled pants; his double chin. If their was a saving grace to his entire appearance, then it was his tie, a checked one that was obviously the tartan of some Scottish clan. It brightened up his face so much, that everything above his neck appeared to be gift-wrapped. Everything below, seemed to be shabby, over-sized, and about to burst out of it's brown paper wrapping. If, against all of Sissy's expectations, he was the author of *The Portrait of a Lady*, then she had been mistaken about him being a genius, he was a buffoon.

"Dear, Mister James" Sissy offered her hand.

"Lady Shum" replied Henry with a little bow "you look delightful."

"Enchanté ..." Sissy countered, determined to not let slip her brogue.

"Parlez-vous Francais, madmoiselle?" Henry asked.

"Oui, mais ma Latin est better" she answered with a laugh. She wondered how he would react to her bad French, for he looked very stern and serious, and just for a moment she thought he was about to tilt his head and look at her in a condescending, patronising manner. But he did not, he laughed too.

"I much prefer English, don't you?" he asked in an accent that was more English than the English. There was hardly a trace of an American accent.

"I like the Irish myself" Sissy joked "but there's not so many in London could keep up with it. Have you been to Ireland, Henry."

"Indeed I have" he laughed at Sissy calling him Henry. There, he thought, was a sign of the new younger generation, less formal, friendlier, and immediately willing to be intimate. If anything, by choosing to live in England, he missed the instant familiarity that was so common in America. He had found a similar friendliness in Ireland, and pleasantly discovered that people were genuinely interested in him because he was a foreigner. In England, all foreigners were treated with some suspicion, hence his need, in order to succeed socially, his recourse to adopting English dress, manners, and speech. Now, adjusting to the fact that Lady Shum had spent her entire life in Ireland, and appeared to possess all the endearing qualities that so marked the Irish in Boston, he at once felt a kinship with the pleasant looking creature that stood smiling before him. "Am I to call you Elizabeth, then?"

Sissy swallowed a little and whispered in his ear "Absolutely not! Everyone knows me as Sissy." She handed him the box of ties.

"Ah ha!" declared Henry out loud. "Empress by name, empress by nature" he laughed opening the box. He was delighted with the ties. He glanced at Clarissa. "My god! It's

.... isn't it?" He took her hand and kissed it. "Why didn't you say" he uttered in disbelief. "I was told that .... "

He stopped short. His mind began to swim with memories of the weeks that had followed the arrival of Olive Vanya back from Washington. During her stay in the James house, and before her departure for Ireland, Henry had fallen in love with Clarissa. They had had intercourse in the kitchen when Henry had come down from his room late at night for a glass of milk and found Clarissa slumped across the kitchen table crying. She confided that she was not looking forward to going to Ireland as she had grown to love America and wished to remain. Henry tried to encouraged her to follow her feelings, but she said she could not leave her mistress at such a bad time. He had comforted her by putting his arms around her, but they were young, and the embrace turned into a frenzied half-hour of tongues, sweat and orgasm. They openly continued their liaison up until Clarissa's departure for Ireland with Olive Vanya, even though it was thoroughly frowned upon by Henry Senior, who would have preferred his son to comfort Olive Vanya rather than the maid. Olive Vanya had also disapproved of the liaison as it threatened to take Clarissa from her, but in the end, her fears proved groundless. Clarissa left with her, and Henry was left pouring his heart out to his little sister Alice.

However, there was one unforeseen complication. Clarissa had borne Henry a child. While Olive Vanya's child had been premature, Clarissa's had been a month overdue. The overlap had been a little less than one month, yet no-one had noticed Clarissa's condition, naturally assuming that she was overweight. She had by sheer will managed to delay the birth of her own child until after the burial of Olive Vanya's in the crypt. She had faked going to Cashel to grieve the loss of her mistress, in reality, she had instead gone to Dublin and given birth to a daughter. There she fed the baby herself for a month, then arranged for the child to taken as an orphan to the convent of The Sisters of Mary, where on the same day she returned and asked the then Mother Superior to admit her to the sisterhood. They had noted that she had lost a considerable amount of weight, due they thought, to her grieving.

She was shown her own baby, whom the nuns described to her as being abandoned, and they let her hold the child. The child had snuggled into her swollen breasts, but she could not feed it for fear of being discovered full of milk. The child had cried when they had taken it from her, and would not stop crying until they had placed it back in her arms. The Mother Superior was told of this, and mindful of her way with the child, put Clarissa in charge of all the convent's small children, including Sissy.

Left much of the time alone with Sissy and her own daughter, she would breast feed both at the same time, supplementing their bottled cow's milk with her own. Thus it was later, that although Clarissa devoted much of her energies bringing up the daughter of Olive Vanya, she managed in quiet moments to spend time with her own child, Marion. It was by some mistake that Marion was judged to be two months younger than Sissy, when in fact Sissy was only two weeks older, for the nuns had agreed that Marion looked as though she had just been born when she was brought to the convent.

All these years later, Clarissa was re-meeting the father of her child. Deep down she had dreamed of being able to do so with her daughter, and now, at last, it was so. For Clarissa had switched the children, substituted her own child as the heiress of the Rostov fortune. At first she had not intended to do it, but as the months went by, and Clarissa repeatedly called the children by each other's name, the other nuns came to know Clarissa's child as Elizabeth and the real Elizabeth as the abandoned child Marion. It had not seemed possible to do, nor had there been any real reason for Clarissa to do it, but nevertheless, she had achieved it.

"Hello, Henry" Clarissa grimaced as he kissed her on the hand. "How are you?"

She asked the question in such a matter of fact way, Henry felt that there was something wrong. She had aged, they both had, but he had always remembered her as a happy outgoing kind of girl. Now, she looked nothing more than a dried up old spinster whose hair was so short it looked like a man's. In contrast, the young Lady Shum shone like a jewel.

"Lets go to dinner!" declared Henry taking the arm of Clarissa.

Sissy was furious as she found herself trailing gangly along behind the older couple as they left the hotel. She could barely hide her contempt. She begrudged the attention Henry James was showing to Clarissa. She was her maid! She had stolen her escort for the night. She would find a way later of punishing Clarissa for ruining her evening.

7

Marion's cell was so small that there was only just room for her, a tiny chest-of-drawers and a prie-dieu, a chair, a minute folding table and a hard little bed. Drawers, doors and windows had to be opened noiselessly. She had been long accustomed to the rough woollen sheets that were washed only once a year. There was no washstand; instead a small earthen jug and basin stood in a corner on the floor. Bare floorboards and plain-whitewashed walls intensified the atmosphere of austerity. None were allowed to enter her cell except the Superior, or the nun who held the office of apothecary in the event of illness.

The day after Sissy had left, Marion had decided to give up being a lay sister postulant and become a nun proper. Outsiders often imagine that girls go into convents because of unsuccessful love affairs, some do, but they are rare. Marion did not feel as though God had chosen her, nor did she have a craving for contact with

God, but she was naturally devout. Marriage did not particularly attract her; she liked saying her prayers rather than praying; and she loved the quiet, well-ordered existence of the convent, with heaven as its goal. There were certainly other novices who had come from the outside world ready to trample underfoot everything in order to make contact with God. They were possessed by a burning hunger and thirst for God. They knew him not as some vague, remote, spiritual ideal, but a living person.

The Mother Superior had her doubts about Marion's suitability for the Order. She decided to admit Marion on a probationary period before admitting her as a full novice, for Marion was extremely lively and very attached to her own way at looking at things. The first thing that the Mistress of Novices explained to her was the importance of being exact about even the smallest details of the Rules of Modesty.

"You must give up your own tastes and habits and allow the Rule to mould you according to the pattern of the Order."

Marion was very familiar with the Rules, but she had never been compelled to abide by them every second of the day. As a prospective novice she now found that when walking she was not allowed to swing her arms. Instead, she had to meekly keep them clasped together at the level of her waist. To hurry was another breach of decorum. She was obliged to take short, measured steps, head bent a little forward and eyes cast down. This custody of the eyes was considered so important that to raise them, even for a moment, without strict necessity, in choir or refectory, was a breach of the Rule.

"God is a Spirit" said the Novice Mistress "he is everywhere - but for us he can only be contacted in the centre of our souls."

"Centre of our souls?" asked Marion.

"The deepest, innermost part of you, the central core of your personality. This is where the real adventures of spiritual life take place. The difficulty is how to get there." She fingered the crucifix dangling from her neck. "There is only one way to get there - by recollection. You must shut off everything from your mind that is external, so that your mind might be free from all external thoughts. By introversion your mind can enter itself and concentrate on its own deepest part. You must go on and on emptying your mind of thoughts and images so that your facilities are kept free from memory, thought and desire." The Novice Mistress gave Marion a book called Of Union with God "I'll talk with you in two weeks time and see how you are progressing."

Marion read the little book that explained that it was of the greatest importance that what has been seen, heard, done or said, should not leave traces in the imagination. To arrive at emptiness of mind, she was to bar the door to her senses, guard her heart against all images and shapes of earthly things, draw her powers inwards, and then lift them up to God.

She tried. Day after day she concentrated

on developing an inward habit of trying to efface from her memory every kind of impression. Her custody of the eyes was so rigorous she became a menace to the community, for she constantly bumped into people who happened to be coming her way.

Yet, no matter how hard she tried, she could not succeed in erasing any thoughts at all. If anything, the denial of the outside world led her to crave it all the more. As she shut herself away in her cell, outside in the dormitory, habited figures moved up and down like shadows. Not a sound broke the stillness - neither the sound of voices or passing feet.

The convent was very large. Built round a small fifteenth century courtyard, it had grown with the centuries until it lay like a long, grey sleeping reptile, clutching four other courtyards and a cloister between its claws. In winter, the cold cut through the convent like a knife. The damp light crept in through the deep-sill, lead glass windows and froze immediately on the whitewashed walls. Out in the cloister, the heavy oak doors hid the rabbit warren of kitchen rooms; hospital; school; boarding house; refectory; community room; library; chapel; and the great damp vaults below.

It would take considerable time to describe the entire whole of the convent, the Refectory's unglazed paintings of the Nativity, the Adoration of the Magi, the Marriage of St. Catherine, or the tragic canvases of the Crucifixion with weeping angels holding chalices beneath the wounds of the tortured Christ. Nothing there had been changed since it was built three hundred years before; the same thick-paned latticed windows overlooked the same high-walled garden; the same bare oak tables were set with the same plates of dinted pewter and brown earthen mugs; spiritual intensity hung in the air like some delicate, distilled fragrance from another world. In the Community Room, the living room of the nuns stood an ugly, carved altar with twisted barley-sugar columns and an array of aspidistras clutching for light from the long row of high windows that were always closed. Beneath the windows, set close together in a long line were a series of narrow oak tables where a hundred or more nuns could sit comfortably side by side. Against the walls, a row of heavy rush-woven chairs alternated with plain oak cupboards and massive chests with coffin-like drawers in which the nuns could keep their books and work. Above, like vultures gazing down on them, the canvas portraits of the twenty five or more Prioresses who had ruled the convent since its sacking by zealots in 1537. Here the nuns could sit sewing from nine until eleven, half past one till three, or again from four till five. It was place of suffering, and until the spiritual had triumphed over what was merely natural, suffering could not be avoided. After all, suffering was the price of sanctity. After supper, the community assembled in the Community Room for recreation. The Prioress, and Mother Superior Gabriella, sat at the long row of tables with the nuns down either side. The rule of silence no longer held; the walls echoed with laughter and conversation. It was the nun's sanctuary from God, a room so large that even when the entire community of five hundred was assembled, it never seemed crowded.

However, the largest room in the convent was the Library. It was here that Marion spent much of her two weeks in novice preparation reading Didon's *Life of Christ*, St. Bernard's *Canticle of Canticles*, and a host of other religious texts. It was by chance that she came upon a book hidden away in the recesses of a shelf stuck in the furthest corner from the door.

"The Origin of the Species" she whispered to herself "by Charles Darwin, M.A., F.R.S." At first she merely dusted it off and thought to put it back on the shelf, but curiosity got the better of her, and she opened it and began to look at the illustrations. Then she began to read the text, and for all of what seemed like an hour scanned, and flipped, and read things that made her break out into a cold swear in case she was discovered. She re-hid the book on a shelf higher up, and with downcast eyes, walked back to her cell to think about what she had read.

How had that book got there? she asked herself. It was certainly not a religious book, in fact, it was a most irreligious book. How could men be descended from apes. God had made Adam, Adam had made Eve, and so on, and so forth ....

That night Marion could not sleep. When

the heavy iron bell of the Caller rang and she opened the door of her cell to call 'Deo gratiases', Marion was already washed and dressed. She tried to blot out Darwin's book by recollection and introversion, but she could not. She returned to the library as soon as breakfast and morning prayers were over, and resumed reading where she had left of the day before, but it was not long before another nun disturbed her.

"Have you seen The Cloud of Unknowing?" she was asked.

"Eh, I have not" she answered nervously.

"What about St. Thomas's *Summa Contra Gentilium*?"

"St. Thomas's what?" Marion said vacantly.

The nun looked at her strangely, but said nothing further, and passed on to another row of shelves.

Marion decided that it was too dangerous to read in public the book she had found. She decided to conceal it in her clothing and smuggle it out of the library to her cell. Unfortunately, fourteenth century ascetics had contrived the garments, which she had to rearrange to hide the book. She was wearing a thick, long sleeved shift of rough, scratchy serge next to her skin, which reached to her ankles. A stay, severely boned and shoulder strapped, concealed the contours of her body, over which, two long serge petticoats were lashed securely round her waist. On top of this was a habit-coat of ample heavy cloth, topped by a linen rochet and a stiffly starched barbette of cambric, folded into a score of tiny tucks and pleats at the neck. On her legs were enormous stockings, far thicker than those used by men to tramp the moors, and shrunk by repeated boiling to the shape and consistency of Wellington boots. There was nowhere to hide the book without it showing unless she tucked it into the top of one of her thick stockings. She hiked up her skirts and pushed the book into a stocking on the inside of her thigh. It felt very uncomfortable, but if she walked slowly, with her hands clasped at the waist, and took very small steps, the binding of the book did not chaff her leg too severely. Thus, with custody of the eyes, she walked at a snail's pace out of the Library, past the Community Room, Refectory and kitchens, until in the shadows of the dormitory, the book fell out of her stocking and on to the stone floor.

The noise the book made as it fell sounded like thunder to Marion in the silent atmosphere of the Dorm. Marion froze, the book hidden by her skirts, daring neither to bend to pick it up, or to abandon it in the shadows. At last she decided she would risk picking it up, for none had noticed, and certainly none would ask her any questions about possessing a library book. She swooped and scooped the book into her hand, but as she did so, the Novice Mistress entered the Dorm and saw her. She approached, looked at the spine of the book, seized it, and in a fit of gesticulation, indicated that Marion was to follow her out of Dorm and straight to the room of the Prioress.

Needless to say, Prioress Gabriella was

firstly shocked, angry, and then disappointed to discover that such a book had been found in the Library. She ordered the entire library to be searched for blasphemous books. In the meanwhile, Marion was severely censured.

"I am most disappointed in you, girl. You should have reported it immediately. Didn't your common sense tell you that it was a banned book?"

"I am sorry, Reverend Mother" she said with custody of the eyes.

"Taking of books out of the Library without signing for them is offence enough, but the smuggling of one in your underclothes is deceitful and totally without defence. The Novice Mistress tells me that you have had difficulty with recollection and introversion?"

"I have tried, Reverend Mother." This time she looked up at Prioress Gabriella "but I don't think I will ever be able to do it."

Gabriella knew the situation was hopeless. Years of convent training had taught her to recognise when to let one of the flock go, but she could not bring herself to do it.

"We'll put you back to work in the school for awhile. With a world full of food shortages, political upheaval, and a rising cost of living, it's no place for a young girl. You're fortunate you have somewhere, girl. I have letters from Sissy Shum wanting to know if you'll be joining her in London. I do not approve of her fondness for you. You'd been showing promise as a novice, and up 'til now, I've not allowed any of her letters to reach you." Gabriella held up a half-a-dozen letters from Sissy. "As it is, you are close to Sissy and Sister Bonaventure, and it would not be right for me to keep you from the only family you have known." She passed the letters over to Sissy. "However, on the matter of the book, you will have to confess your sins to Father McNabb, write to the Bishop for forgiveness, and pray that we don't receive a visit from the Cardinal."

However, three days later, Cardinal Manning appeared at the long polished table in the Community Room. His Monsignor and the Prioress flanked him. Marion, re-assigned to the school, sat at the back of the room with the convent children. She had read Sissy's fanciful scribbling about how wonderful Dublin and London were, and found as she read each letter in turn, how Sissy seemed to become further and further away. The world appeared to be changing her, and Marion did not particularly like Sissy's references to the men she had met.

As his Grace began to deliver his talk to the nuns about the danger of the written word, a mother mouse, followed by her family of little mouselings, appeared suddenly from nowhere and marched with a bounce and a purpose across the floor. The spectacle of the creatures marching single-file was so unexpected that that the nuns either shrieked or laughed. The Cardinal paused until the procession passed. However, when Marion bent down to pray, she discovered one of the little mouselings taking refuge in the folds of her skirt. It made no effort to move, so she picked it up and took it with her back to her cell. She fancied that it was the runt of the litter, for it was the thinnest mouse she had ever seen. It lay in the palm of her hand without any desire to escape. She was wondering how she could feed it, when she heard the tings sounding for her. Each member of the community had their own combination of knocks and tings on the two six inch bars of steel that hung in the cloister, and had to call out in a loud voice deo gratias when summoned.

"Deo gratias!" shouted Marion.

Mouse in hand; she went forth to discover that the Cardinal had sent for her. She could not think what to do with the mouse, so she took it with her. The Cardinal examined it with quiet interest when she shepherded it very carefully through the grille which always separated the clergy from the nuns. The Cardinal returned it to her.

"And to think there are people who refuse to believe in the existence of God. If that were the case, how could anything so delicate and perfectly made be unless it were the concept of an infinite mind?"

Marion dared not tell the Prince of the Church what was in her mind. "Yes, your Grace" she replied.

"God has taken a human body with which to do his work on earth. Just as nineteen hundred years ago, God, taking Christ's human body, was born and lived and taught and suffered and died and rose again from the dead, so today we go along doing just the same things in a body formed out of the living members of the

Church. We, through our sufferings, have God continuing in our own person, living out the agony and the passion of the Crucified. Are you with me, Sister?"

"Yes, your Grace." The little mouse was wriggling in her hands.

"One's own body, for example, has its own bodily life, unique and simple ... but inside that body there are innumerable cells which make up that life. Each of these cells lives separately by its own individual life, but also contributes to the unity of the body as a whole. Well, the same thing applies to that body in which God lives today. It too consists of such a unity of cells, each a human entity, separate and complete in itself, yet at the same time, a cell in the very Body of Christ. Thus Christ still lives upon earth in the persons who truly keep his commandments. The Church is quite simply Christ himself."

Marion could not quite grasp the Cardinal's meaning. "But are we really apes?" she asked hesitantly.

"Though Mister Darwin has demonstrated that genetically we may be descended from apes, he has not touched upon the concept of God's living body. It is unreasonable to expect non-human creatures to take on the work of God, and therefore we must exclude them from his living body. Even if we include them, we return to the age old question - who created the Heavens and Earth? The Origin of Species does not answer anything it only creates more questions. We are no wiser about the existence of God by knowing that we are descended from apes. We are no better comforted by the knowledge that eruptions or deposits of silt formed rocks. Only by searching to the inner core of our own beings, by recollection and introversion can you become truly united to God. Naturally, the Church must devote some lives to the service of mankind, missionary work, teaching, nursing the sick, but the hidden life of contemplation has always held first place. Teaching, preaching, nursing, missionary work and so on makes up the public life of the Body, but behind this are the power houses, the great contemplative orders, Cathusians, Cistercians, Carmelites, Benedictines and the likes of your own convent which by their hidden lives of prayer and penance supply God's dynamic spiritual force. The help they bring to the world is unlimited. People who are truly united to God are at the white-hot centre of the furnace ... at the very source of that Infinite, Absolute Force, that creates and preserves the world. It may be said, in a certain sense, that they control It. When God raises a soul to the highest degree of contemplation, he refuses it nothing, so that such a soul is in a position to do really miraculous things for the salvation and sanctification of the world. It is this that is granted so often to the prayers of the saints ...."

The Cardinal kept Marion on the other side of the grille for almost an hour, explaining the workings of the Mystical Body of Christ, until at the end of the interview, Marion was drained and repentant, and made well aware that she had misinterpreted her calling, and had fallen to the servitude of mankind, and not Christ.

She returned to cell depressed and empty with the little mouse, which weak and hungry, died in the night.

8

With the constraints of the convent lifted from them, the orderly relationship that had previously existed between Sissy and Clarissa crumbled. It soon became apparent that their new lady-maid situation would not work. Times had changed and Sissy felt it a constant embarrassment to be accompanied by Clarissa, for she felt her to be old, argumentative, and stubborn, refusing to allow her the freedom Sissy felt was due to her as a Lady.

Clarissa, for her part, was not willing to let her own daughter treat her as a common household servant. She resented her own wasted years in the convent, and this resentment was directed at Sissy whenever she was angered by her daughter's ingratitude.

Their time in London was intense. Sissy had 'befriended' a gentleman in the hotel and had gone to his room un-chaperoned where she had remained for the night. The following night she did the same, but with a different man. Clarissa was livid, and when her daughter returned to their room early the next morning, she caught hold of her and slapped her hard across the face.

"You whore!" she cried, hitting her again

and again.

"Leave me alone, you witch! Leave me!" she screamed.

"You're a dirty little trollop!" She laid hold of Sissy's low cut corset and pulled at it so hard that it ripped and her large breasts fell out. She grabbed hold of her nipples with her fingers and pinched them hard. Sissy screamed the roof down. "That will teach you, you little bitch!"

Clarissa let go of Sissy's nipples and tried to slap her across the face again, but Sissy fell against the end of Clarissa's bed and found herself lying on the bedspread. In an instant, she grabbed the chamber pot under the bed, and tried to throw it at Clarissa. The contents went all over the bed. In a rage, Clarissa threw herself on Sissy, and as they struggled on the bed, Clarissa managed to put her hands round Sissy's neck, squeezing ever tighter and tighter.

"Stop it, Bonny ... Stop it ....." she choked, pounding on Clarissa's arms with her fists. As the air went out of her, she clutched at the soiled bedspread. She could barely smell the staleness of Clarissa's urine, for no air was reaching her.

Clarissa continued to squeeze and squeeze with arms that had done a life of heavy tasks and duties. She wished to teach her young daughter a lesson she would remember, scare her so much that she would never sleep with a strange man again. She wanted to see the girl's face turn blue and her eyes go red with fear. Her going with men was the work of the devil, she told herself. She shook Sissy by the neck until she stopped struggling, and when all resistance had ceased, she released her and told her to get up.

Sissy did not get up. She lay lifeless on the bed. "Get up, Sissy!" she ordered again.

She turned her back on her and went to wash in the hand basin. She ran the hot water, she looked in the mirror expecting to see her daughter move or make a noise. She carried on washing her hands over and over in the warm water until the mirror steamed over. As she dried her hands on a towel she began to tremble. She had begun to hear voices, the same voices that had come to her all those years ago when she had first entered the convent. It was the voices that had told her to switch the babies. Through recollection and intro-version she had made the voices go away, but now they were back, telling her what to do, what to say.

"Come, Sissy, we said we would go to see the Tower today."

She went to the wardrobe and selected her clothes for the day. Perhaps, she would try wearing a corset, to push her breasts up and out like Sissy's. She had ample breasts herself, and now she would show them. "What do you think, liebling?" she asked.

She went over to the bed and saw her daughter motionless. "You must be tired after being up all night." She wrapped the bedspread round Sissy, carried on dressing, and went downstairs for breakfast as if nothing had happened.

*

When Henry had arrived Liverpool, it was just about that time in November when autumn changed to winter. In New England, the arrival of winter was marked by snow, but in England, winter crept up on the country like the ebb and flow of the in-coming tide. Just as one thought that it had arrived, it would receed again, so that one could never be certain if the sun would shine or the wind would blow.

Henry had hired a nurse to meet the arriving Americans. They were up early to embrace his exhausted sister on board ship at seven-thirty in the morning. It was necessary to have her carried off the ship and to his hotel. It distressed him to discover that his sister's wilful mind was encased in a feeble body, and although Katherine Loring was her first line of support, she could not be with her constantly.

After leaving Boston ill, Alice had become further ill at sea.

"It was terrible, Henry ... I had a rather tragic time" she wheezed between bouts of coughing and spitting. "Katherine has been more devoted to me than ever. She was heroic."

Henry's first impression of Katherine Loring had been confounded two years earlier when he had met her. She was the daughter of a wealthy Boston family. She was the director of an educational college teaching history to women by correspondence, and was an adamant campaigner for the rights of women. She had employed Alice and had been delighted in her achievements as a teacher, adding a sharp pen and a useful resourcefulness to the work of her education program.

Small, bespectacled, mousy, yet energetic, Katherine and Alice quickly became intimate friends, bewildering the James family, and leading Henry and the wife of his brother William, to speculate about the erotic nature of Katherine Loring long before they ever met her. Henry had imagined her to be some Amazonian giant, striding through life as the champion of women's causes, but when he finally met her, he was disappointed by her physical presence, for she certainly did not look as though she could shoot a rifle. However, within minutes, he realised he was mistaken, for the force of her personality quickly made him realise that she was capable of everything Alice had said she was. In the end he had declared that Katherine was the most perfect companion Alice could have found.

"Alice" interjected Katherine "is not well enough at present to go on to London, and not well enough to be in lodgings on her own."

"She can't be with me" said Henry. It was obvious that Katherine Loring was intending to go off on one of her lecturing tours. "I have no room for her maid, or the resources." Henry was hard-up for cash, he could ill-afford his sister descending on him. He would never be able to get on with The Bostonians.

"Very well, then" Katherine said angrily "After she's rested two or three days here, I shall take her to Bournemouth to the same house as my sister Louise!"

Henry felt miserable. He was not been willing to help his frail sister. He had not thought about the length and extent of his responsibility now that their parents were dead. Under the impression that his sister had come to England to live with the Lorings, he now knew this to be a false pretext, and that his sister had no intention of returning to America. He was expected to be her practical support and empathetic visitor during her various illnesses, her improvements, her relapses, her disappointments, for it was obvious that Katherine Loring, however devoted to Alice, had her own life to lead. Certainly, she would take her to Bournemouth, but how long would it be before they had to find her somewhere else?

"I met the delightful Lady Shum, Alice." Henry told her everything. "Clarissa was there too."

"Not the same Clarissa?" Alice wheezed.

"The very same."

"Are you still in love with her?" she quizzed

"Of course not. It was all so long ago. She's old and wrinkled, and anyway, you know I have this new friend I wrote to you about."

"The painter?"

"Wonderfully talented! I met him in Paris. I will let you meet him next time he comes to London. He's going to paint my portrait."

Henry looked at Alice lying on her bed. He had hoped she would come to England healthy, and that he could escape the responsibility of caring for her. But he knew it would not be so. He would have to be with her and available to her, as she desired, and always, even if it meant moving to Bournemouth.

When Henry James returned to London with his sister (for he had relented to have her stay in his rented rooms in Bolton Street), he opened the morning paper to read of the murder in the Savoy. He immediately took a cab to Bow Street Police Station where he was admitted to see Clarissa Blum.

"She might be a bit disturbed, sir" the desk sergeant warned him. "One minute she's fine, the next as loony as you can get."

He was ushered by a policeman into a small cell with a narrow wooden bed and a chamber pot in the corner. There were six-inch bars on a high single window. Clarissa sat on the end of the bed.

"Hello, Clarissa ....."

She did not look up. She had fallen back on her convent 'custody' of her eyes. He knelt down to look into her eyes, but she threw herself across her bed.

"Go away, please. Please, go away."

Henry got the impression that she wanted to cry but that she could not. He sat on the edge of the bed and laid his hand on her shoulder.

"I'm here to help." His immediate first thought was whether she had a legal man to defend her.

"I'm guilty. I killed my own daughter." The utterance of the words cut into Henry's soul like an razor.

"I know Sissy was like a daughter to you ..." He tried to comfort her.

"She was my own daughter" Clarissa stated tragically.

"Your own daughter?" Henry was bewildered. Indeed, she was disturbed. She had cared for Sissy so long that she had come to believe her to be her own daughter. "And your daughter, Henry." She laid her hand on his.

Henry James thought back to those days in Boston. Yes, it had been twenty two years ago? Sissy was twenty-one. No, it was possible, yet the dates fitted. Sissy was his own daughter? He could still see her face in his mind. Yes, there was a resemblance - the forehead, the nose, the same down-turned mouth. Surely not?

Clarissa lifted herself and began to tell Henry the whole story of the babies, how she had been mentally ill, how she had gone on pretending Sissy was Olive Vanya's daughter when in fact she was her own.

"She wouldn't do as she was told" she explained. "She never did what she was told, even when she was a child. She always laughed at me, answered back to me. I scolded her, and she still laughed, called me a Penguin! It was hurtful. I would twist her arm until she cried, but she would remain defiant, calling me names. I hated her. I was her mother but I couldn't tell her. She had the devil in her! Oh, how she hid it when there were others around, all sweet and innocent, but the other children knew, Marion knew. I would care for them both and Marion would be grateful and kind in return, but Sissy, she was always spiteful, always vicious. I wished that Marion were my daughter and not Sissy, but she was not, and perhaps had I not switched the babies, then my own life in the convent would have been a happy one. I did a wrong thing. I wanted my own daughter to grow up and be like the Countess Olive Vanya, inherit the wealth that awaited her at twenty-one, and for years, it was this one thought that kept me going. I was overjoyed to receive my rescript and leave the convent behind. It was a prison; a living nightmare of dullness and austerity, and how I prayed for the day my daughter would inherit the fortune and set me up in luxury. I had seen how the wealthy lived their idle lives, being served by the likes of me, and I wanted that for myself. If it involved twenty years of religious imprisonment to come into a fortune, then I would surely wait. But I had not taken into account my daughter's nature. I was not willing to be abandoned just days before she came into the Rostov fortune. For that was in her mind, she told me as much the night before I killed her. I saw her go off with that young man to his room and knew that within weeks of her inheriting the fortune, she would have squandered it on men who would steal and deceive her out of every penny. I was incensed. All night I paced the room waiting for her to return, to tell her that I was her real mother, and that unless she turned over the fortune to me for safekeeping, I would expose her as a fraud. As it was, by the time she returned to the room in the morning smelling of sex and alcohol, I was so worked-up with hatred. I flew at her. I could not stop myself. Even when she pleaded with me to stop, I could not. All my plans had fallen to pieces, and I hated her for ruining my life. I strangled her. I knew what I was doing. I do not regret it and I shall go to the gallows. She was my bastard child, and she did not deserve to have the Rostov fortune."

"But she was only a child" Henry reasoned "your one and only child. Did she not have the right to know? Might she not have fallen into your arms, once she knew you were her real mother?"

"Just because I gave birth to her? She would have been even more ungrateful, have hated me even more because I had allowed her to be brought up in a convent. No, she was already on the road to hell. See, you forget that I had two children. One was lost, but there was still time to save the other one from a life of misery in a convent. I had an obligation to Olive Vanya, to bring up her child as best I could. I did this, and the guilt I felt as we left her at the convent gates was so overwhelming I almost turned back. Marion had always been more like a daughter to me than Sissy, and I abandoned her. Sissy loved her, adored her, and had seduced her to be her lover, a common occurrence in the convent. But as soon as we were away from the convent, Sissy forgot all about Marion. I could not. In Dublin Sissy took up with a boy, a nice boy, but it irked me to think that she had put Marion completely out of her thoughts. But this was Sissy's nature;

she was thoughtless and always pursued the moment. She never had any thought for tomorrow, and even less for yesterday."
"But still, you should have told her you were her mother." Henry was irate. He had never wished to be a father, but now that he had discovered that Sissy had been his daughter, he became a grieving father. He cried.
"Oh, Henry" consoled Clarissa "what have you lost? She turned out bad and would have been a worry and an embarrassment to you."
Henry was angry at Clarissa's matter-of-factness "How can you talk like that unless you are totally mad! There was nothing wrong with the girl!"
"She deserved it!" Clarissa had absolutely no remorse. "I gave her life, so it was mine to take away!" Then suddenly, as if the shutters of a bright room were closed to blot out the light, Clarissa began to shake, and tap her hand on the bed.
"Are you all right" asked Henry, but he got no reply. She began to mumble. "Clarissa?" he said trying to attract her attention.
"Yes, Lord ..." she mouthed with trembling lips. She was staring at the wall "Yes, Lord ..." she said over and over again.
The policeman, in attendance close by, indicated with a twirl of his hand that she was mad.
"You'll have nothing more out of her now, sir. I'd call it a day."
On the way out, the desk sergeant told him that he was not sure yet were she would be convicted of first degree murder or

manslaughter on grounds of being unbalanced at the time.

"It's up to the jury, isn't it, sir? The question is did she or did she not know what she was doing?"

Henry nodded his head. He knew she had, but for no logical reason. He felt completely drained. He went for a drink in a nearby pub, then returned to Bolton Street and to the lodgings of his sister to tell her the awful story.

*

The story of the 'Rostov Babies' was leaked to the press by a copper. The newspapers had a field day. They went to town on the fact that Clarissa had been a nun. The Church was ridiculed, and the rich and titled horrified that the murder took place in The Savoy. Interest particularly centred on whether the dead girl was the true heiress to the Rostov fortune or not.

Cardinal Manning visited Reverend Mother Gabriella again. While he was telling her what he had read in the papers, she was informed simultaneously by telegrams from Alice James and by the solicitors Fletcher, Son & Fearnell, and warned about the barrage of reporters that were likely to descent on her convent in Meath. Wisely, the Cardinal ordered the gates of the convent to be locked and no one permitted to enter or leave, and after some discussions with Gabriella, allowed her to go to London with Marion immediately.

Because of the serious implications that the publicity had for the Catholic Church,

Cardinal Newman, primate of England, provided Gabriella and Marion with accommodation in London. Marion, confused, kept asking when she would be seeing Sissy and Sister Bonaventure, until at last, Gabriella could no longer keep the secret from her.

"There's been a terrible accident, my dear."

"What sort of accident?" She knew it had to be serious or they would have rushed off to London without any kind of preparation.

"Sissy has passed away."

"Where has she gone?" asked Marion.

"To heaven, my dear. She is in good hands."

"Oh, I see" replied Marion. She thought about it for a little while. "Where's Sister Bonaventure?"

"She's helping the police to ... " Gabriella could not finish the sentence. The tragedy of the whole situation was almost too much to bear. It made her question God, and why he had allowed such a thing to happen.

Marion had never seen the Reverend Mother so distressed. All during the journey she had fingered her rosary over and over until her fingers were raw. On the train from Liverpool, Marion had caught a headline about a former nun who had killed her love child. She had not been sure what this had meant, but she had overheard two women gossiping in the passage about how the nun had done it for the money. The presence of the Reverend Mother had obviously brought the subject to the fore for the two women, for they kept looking at her and whispering as she stared out the window at the grimy skyline of industrial Manchester.

In London, Marion decided to find out for herself what was going on. On the pretext of going for a walk, she read a newspaper at a stall, and fainted when she discovered that Clarissa had murdered Sissy.

When she regained consciousness, she found herself surrounded by a crowd of concerned people.

"Are you ol'right, Miss?" asked a policeman.

"Where am I?"

"London, Miss" replied the Bobbie in an unmistakable Cockney accent.

"Oh" she uttered in a daze.

"Wot's your name, Miss?"

"Marion"

"Ah, you're a colleen, Miss?" the policeman smiled. "My mum was Irish. Where you lodged then?"

Marion could not remember the name of the Cardinal's house.

"You come with me, Miss. We'll give you a cup of char at the station. You'll be right in mo after a cup of char."

Marion did not argue. She was still weak from the shock. The policeman led her to the police station in Bow Street.

"Out the way there" commanded the policeman as he pushed past a group of men smoking cigarettes on the steps of the station. "Haven't you newspaper men got wives to go home to?"

"Who's this then, Bill?" one of the reporters asked with a smirk. "Another streetwalker you've taken a shine to?"

The reporters and photographers laughed,

for they were happy to have a break from the monotony of hanging about the police station waiting for developments in the Nun story. One of the photographers let off his flash.

"Less of that. This young lady has done nothing wrong. She's a poor Irish girl who's lost her way."

"Irish is she?" inquired another reporter. "You know Sister Bonny the Fortune Killer, then?" he asked jokingly.

Marion's head began to swim. She tottered on the steps and was prevented from falling down them by the policeman. Some of the reporters helped him to carry her inside.

"Get the smelling salts, Sarge!" he shouted.

The reporters and cameramen swarmed round Marion. They sensed a story.

"Where did you find her, Bill?" they asked him.

"Near Cardinal Newman's residence" he said almost involuntary.

"What's her name?"

"She said it was Marion."

The smelling salts were placed under Marion's nose by the sergeant..

"Alright, m'girl" said the Sergeant.

"Is Sister Bonny here" she asked deliriously.

"See, I told you" shouted one of the reporters. "She's the other girl. Get her picture."

The newspapermen scrambled to get as close to her as they could, but the Sergeant and Bill pushed them away. Two other constables were called to clear them from the doorway.

"Let us have her story" they shouted. "It's in the public interest. She's the heiress to the Rostov Fortune!"

"You can wait outside for her" answered back the Sergeant. "Now, Miss, Bill'ill get you a cup of tea, while I send for one of our lads from Scotland Yard."

*

The Church had hoped to pull strings and have Sister Bonaventure quietly put away in a sanatorium, but now that the whole story of the 'Rostov Babies' was splashed across the newspapers, they thought they could turn the trial of Sister Bonaventure into a case of good triumphing over evil.

The important point was to show that Sister Bonaventure had mistaken the babies' identities in their infancy, and that a wicked orphan child had convinced an ill Sister Bonaventure she was her mother. They would have it put about that a medical examination had shown Sister Bonaventure to be a virgin. When by chance the orphan child had come into a fortune, having travelled to London to collect it, on being told that a mistake had been made in infancy, rather than lose the fortune, she had attacked her 'mother', and her 'mother' had killed her in self-defence.

This was to be Clarissa's defence as prepared by the Q.C. employed by Cardinal Newman to defend Clarissa. This would do for the secular world, and ultimately she would be seen to be unbalanced and therefore unfit to stand trial. With a little prayer she might be able to transfer to a church sanatorium.

But no matter how much Cardinal Manning discussed the issue with Cardinal Newman by missive, the Mystical Body of Christ could make no satisfactory plea for Sister Bonaventure. One of their numbers had deceived them and brought the whole Church into question.

The fact that the daughter of Olive Vanya - described by them to the Press as a truly spiritual girl who had consented to take her Vows, but who by a twist of fate, found herself an heiress to a yet undisclosed sum - had decided not to enter the community, and thus not given up her wealth to it; and that the Prioress had known all along about the fortune, were small matters that could not be swept under the carpet by the Mystical Body. Gabriella was viewed most at fault, removed as Prioress, and sent to do missionary work in the Congo, while the Bishop of Dublin was retired early.

This was about all the Church could do to limit the damage. Stricter rules would be enforced in future about Sisters being in charge of young children, for it was felt that the Madonna and Child situation of Clarissa and the 'Rostov Babies' might one day occur again.

*

Clarissa was found guilty of murder with diminished responsibility. The death sentence deferred, she was committed to spend the rest of her life in the Colney Hatch sanatorium for the criminally insane.

The body of Sissy was released from the

morgue. As a bastard child, the Church refused to allow her to be placed in one of their churchyards, so she was buried in a plot reserved by the City for the poor. The funeral was attended by Marion, Henry and Alice James, and Reverend Mother Gabriella.

It was a sad affair, but life went on.

9

Fletcher, Son & Fearnell convened a meeting of the Rostov trustees.

The Reverend Mother Gabriella had already been dispatched to the Congo, and her proxy had been transferred to Cardinal Newman. He was the son of banker and had been a protestant in his youth, an Anglican clergyman in his informative years, and a Roman Catholic since middle age. At the age of seventy-eight he was created Cardinal.

John Newman had often found himself at the centre of the most intense disputes in Victorian England. The 'Rostov Babies' scandal was yet another of those often controversial issues that stirred the nation. He felt that he had to see it through to its conclusion.

He interviewed the girl.

"How are you after all the shock?"

"A little better, your Grace. I've been invited to go to Bournemouth." She was not in the least intimidated by Cardinal Newman. She found him to be very pleasant. He was eighty-five years old and walked with a stoop from carrying the cares of the Church on his back all his life.

"Ah, Bournemouth. How I would like to live in Bournemouth. I've spent my last forty years in Birmingham. It's such a dirty, grimy city. I've heard it described as Hell in England. Well, where better is a Prince of God more needed than in Hell?"

Marion smiled.

"Now, let me ask you this. If you were to become suddenly rich beyond your dreams, what would you do with such riches?" He gazed at her with a quizzical raising of his eye-brows. "Think carefully now. Take your time."

Marion knew what the Cardinal was alluding to. "Naturally" she said "I would want to thank the Church for sheltering me and educating me throughout my childhood. I would think that only proper."

"Splendid!" The Cardinal was pleased. "Perhaps you might think of donating a quarter, or even one third of it for the well-being of other orphans here and abroad?" He watched for her reaction, to see if the idea appealed to her.

Marion smiled benignly. She betrayed nothing. How could she? She was too busy thinking about poor Sissy who had finally come a cropper. There had always been something in Sissy's nature that spelled disaster; she had always been disobedient, and mischievous. Sometimes she had gone too far with her joke taking or the things she said, to the extent that she had sometimes sounded evil and possessed. But whatever the circumstance, Clarissa had had no right to murder her.

The Cardinal was content with the smile as an answer. He did not ask Marion any more questions. He concluded that she was of very sound mind, and high moral thought. She was well versed in Latin, knowledgeable of the bible, and had a firm grasp of what was right and wrong. He was well satisfied that she was worthy of her inheritance.

The second trustee was Alice James.

Of her we know. After the shock of the murder, she had moved to Bournemouth, where Katherine and a hired nurse had charge of her. However, while the trial was going on, Katherine went off to Switzerland, and Henry was forced to move to Bournemouth and take rooms near Alice. Because of their past close involvement with Countess Rostov, Marion was invited to stay with Alice, in part so she and Henry could learn something of the niece and daughter they never got to know.

Alice was very ill and weak, but the company of Marion and her brother soon perked her up. The most considerable charms of Bournemouth were the people invalided there. Henry took her to a small picturesque house high on the west cliff, overlooking the sea. There she met Robert Louis Stevenson, a thin, small, dark-haired, dark-moustached tubercular Scotsman, with a witty, glorious sense of humour that soon had her forgetting all about the pending fortune. Here was the writer of *Treasure Island*, a book she adored for the terror that the Black Spot had filled her with when she first read of it. To Henry he was a young, unique, dishevelled, undressed, loveable young fellow, but to Marion he was a genius.

In the Stevenson house on the cliff were an assortment of characters that fascinated Marion. There was Mrs. Stevenson, a Scotch woman who looked remarkably too young to be the mother of Louis; his Californian wife Fanny who was fifteen years older than Louis; and Fanny' son, Bob, who by all accounts was as weak as Louis, and blind. They welcomed Marion with open arms, and while they renamed Stevenson's grandfather's chair the 'Henry James Chair', they renamed Mrs. Stevenson's footstool 'Marion's Poofé', both to honour and to encourage their frequent visits.

"Will you marry, Mari?" Louis asked her jocularly.

"Maybe if I could find a man" she laughed.

"Och, well, if you do, remember marriage is a field of battle, not a bed of roses. Once you marry, there is nothing left to you, not even suicide, but to be good." He had a good appreciation of the psychological mind. "Sometimes, there are two voices in your head, conflicting voices, one wholly good and fair, the other wicked and bad. Is that not so?" Marion nodded. "When you are driven by the battles of marriage, you must never turn to the wicked and bad. People use the term Jekyll and Hyde to describe someone possessed by conflicting voices, but it was not my intention to have the term used merely for the mad and deranged. All of us have split personalities, and sometimes it is only our spouses or our family who can detect it. Personality is never a static thing, it shifts like sand through an hour-glass, making us first top-heavy, then bottom-heavy, alternating backwards and forwards through life."

Comfortable in Bournemouth, away from the horrors of London, Marion remained with the James's, content to visit the Stevenson's or walk on the beach.

Then something extraordinary happened. She met a young girl on the beach who said her name was Valerie. She had just turned sixteen, and was thoroughly bored. She had a tiny dog that was extremely long with little short legs on a lead that she had to tug to get it to move.

"I hate it here. All my mother ever does is sit and read poetry" the young girl said. It was obvious from her dress that her family was very rich. "Verbotten, Heinz!" she shouted at the dog as it tried to urinate on the sea-front railing.

"Is your mother ill, then?" Marion sympathetically.

"She's always been ill. She says she comes here to treat her sciatica but I think she'd be better in Switzerland, or in a madhouse." Heinz had spotted another dog being walked by its owner on the beach. He sat and watched with his tongue hanging out.

"That's not a nice thing to say about your mother." It upset Marion. Valerie had reminded her of Clarissa.

"Well, she is mad. She reads Heine every hour of the day or sits and dreams about her half-finished fairy castle in Corfu. I'm sick of it."

"Come on" said Marion recognising melancholy "It can't be that bad. I'll buy you a sherbet to cheer you up."

Valerie followed Marion to the Arcade where she purchased two lime sherbets.

"Are you German?" asked Marion as they sat on a bench and watching a group of old ladies being coaxed into the water by an athletic health instructor.

"Austrian!" replied Valerie vehemently.

"Mother of Joseph!" returned Marion with a sense of kinship. "My mother was from Vienna, well, some would say. She was a friend of the Empress Elizabeth."

Valerie gave a sudden jolt.

"What's the matter?" asked Marion.

"I'm not supposed to talk to strangers" Her mother had told her to reveal nothing. She stood up in a brisk manner that frightened Marion into dropping her sherbet on to the stone paving of the promenade.

"Look what you've made me do" moaned Marion.

"Heinz! Verbotten! Verbotten!" screamed Valerie at the dog as it began licking the sherbet. She kicked the dog and gave out a squeal and ran under the bench and hid.

"What's the matter with you?" said Marion angrily, pulling the dog from out under the bench, then with a bit of a struggle, setting him on her lap. "You should be nicer to animals. All they want is a bit of love."

"So do I" declared Valerie flopping back on to the bench and crossing her arms. "I'm sick of being shuffled backwards and forwards across Europe. Mama doesn't even ask me if I want to go with her or not. I have to do whatever she says. Papa wants me to be with him, but Mama won't let me. I never see my sister Gisela or brother Rudolf, and I only see Papa when we go for short stays at Godollo or the villa at Lainz. The rest of the time we're in Corfu or England." Valerie turned and pointed "Look, there she is, do you see her? The one with the small lace parasol. That's Mama. Doesn't she look silly?"

Marion looked beyond the railings of the promenade and saw a tall, slender woman dressed in brown alpaca, sitting on the beach alone, staring out to sea, writing, then staring out to sea again.

"She's dreaming about Heine" said Valerie matter-of-factly. "I can always tell when she's think about him."

"Is that right, now. What's she writing then?"

"Probably her own poetry, or a letter to Papa, who knows" Valerie said discursively. "She might even be writing to Queen Victoria. She said she wanted to see her before we went home for Christmas."

Marion's eyes lit up like a child's on Guy Fawkes Night.

"Come, I'll introduce you to Mama." Valerie took the leash and tried to make Heinz jump down from Marion's lap. "Kommen sie, Heinz" she said in a false voice of friendliness.

The dog refused to budge.

"Down, Heinz" ordered Marion, and the animal jumped to ground, taking wide berth

of Valerie's feet. "He seems to understand English. Don't you Heinzey?"
The dog barked as if it understood. Valerie was much more sceptical.
"He's a stupid dog" she said as she led him down the steps that descended to the sands. Heinz tried to run ahead of Valerie, but the leash was too short, and the steps too steep for his small legs. He took fright and tried to run back up the stairs again.
"See what I mean. Stupid!" Valerie picked him and carried him down the rest of the way.
As they approached Valerie's mother across the sands, she turned and watched Valerie release Heinz from his leash. The little sausage dog snaked its way across the sands towards Valerie's mother, and just in time, she put down her writing pad, as the dog jumped onto her lap.
"Where have you been?" The Empress of Austria was obsessive about her youngest daughter. She was the only one of her four children whom she had completely to herself. Her mother-in-law had stolen the others from her, and she had pledged that nobody was going to have any claims on Valerie but her. Without realising it, Valerie was Empress Sisi's only link with reality. The rest of her time she spent in a dream, closed off in a bubble of wealth, castles, and palaces. It was Valerie who jolted her out of the nothingness of living, brought the world to her, for she was incapable of going to the world, and had long given up hope that the world wanted her. However, she was not mad like her uncle Ludwig of

Bavaria who gave firework displays just for himself or mounted Wagner operas in Munich that only he watched.

Elizabeth was still beautiful, more magnificently beautiful in her forties than she was in her twenties. She only had to smile or gesture mildly and she melted hearts. Of late she had been sadder than usual, as she had finally abandoned her constant escort Captain Bay Middleton, the finest horseman in England. He had been her companion for ten years, but it come to an end, as all things came to an end.

Once more alone, Sisi had finally come to realise how alone Franz Josef had been all those years she had left him on his own while she was away travelling, escaping from the claustrophobic Hofburg court. Out of concern for Franz Josef's needs, she had found a companion for her husband, a young actress from the Burgtheater, and by guarding her from gossip, he was able to enjoy young, pleasant company and chatter, home-baking, and sex.

"Mama ... this is Marion" Valerie prompted.

"My real name is Elizabeth Shum .... " Marion replied. It still sounded strange to her after years in the convent being known only as Marion.

"Pleased to meet you, Elizabeth" Sisi said indicating her to sit on the blanket that had been spread out on the sand.

Marion sat on the left side of the Empress, Valerie on the right. Unaware whom Valerie's mother was, as she once more gazed out to sea, Marion was suddenly struck by her beauty. She had never seen a woman look so perfect. There was not a line in her face, not one crease at the mouth or a furrow along her forehead. If she had not known, she might have thought the Empress Valerie's sister. Even her fingers, her delicate artistic fingers escaping from her elbow length fingerless gloves, were so perfectly formed that Marion thought them the most beautiful fingers in all the world. The sculptured fingers of the Madonna in the convent, by contrast, were crude and lifeless, although up until then, she had always thought them beautiful.

"Marion says her mother was from Vienna" Valerie said pouring a little sand on Heinz's head.

"Valerie ..." Sisi ordered her daughter. The dog looked up pleadingly with its little red eyes. "That's enough cruelty to Heinz today. You are always like this when die Regel haben."

Marion picked up what was meant. She had often heard Clarissa use the same term in the convent when she talked about menstruation.

"So your mother was Viennese?" Sisi asked.

"She said her mother knew Empress Elizabeth" Valerie was enjoying the fact that Marion did not know who her mother was.

"Everyone in Vienna claims to know the Empress" laughed Elizabeth.

"She died when I was born. I was told she was an opera singer."

"How fascinating. How did you end up in England?"

"Well, it's a long story." Marion was not sure whether she wanted to get into telling two strangers all about her past and about the fortune she was about to inherit. But she was bursting to tell someone, and Valerie and her mother seemed to be very nice. "My mother and father were really Russian, that's why I look the way I do."

"You are very beautiful"

"Do you think so? I never look in the mirror. In the convent we had no mirrors."

"You did not go to school here?"

"No ... in Ireland."

Suddenly a change came over Valerie's mother. It was as if the pieces of a fragmented day had finally crystallized into a weary sigh, which during the day caused the body to slump and the mind to ponder.

Marion noted the transformation, wondering what had caused the change.

"Mama ... wie es du?" Valerie asked.

"Leave me, Valerie" Sisi silenced her daughter "Let me think ... let me think."

Valerie looked at Marion and raised her eyebrows as if to say 'I told you so'.

"Enough of that" declared Sisi, catching her daughter making faces. "Here, take Heinz for a run along the water."

Valerie rose without further prompting. "Are you coming" she asked Marion.

"No, I wish to speak some more with Elizabeth."

"Okay, Mama ..." Valerie was happy that her mother was talking to someone, for too often she sat for days on her own speaking to no-one. She picked up a rubber play-ball from under the blanket. "Kommst, Heinz."

The dog faithfully followed her across the wet sands to the water's edge some distance away.

The Empress took Marion's right hand and studied it. "I knew your mother. Olive Vanya. Is that not correct?"

"Yes" stuttered Marion. "But when?"

"In Vienna. For some years she was my best friend. I adored her. She was the only one who understood what it was like to be trapped inside a beautiful body."

"You're the most beautiful person I've ever seen." Marion felt she had to say it. The words had been on her lips since she had first sat down on the blanket.

"Yes, and it is a tragedy. You do not know the power I wield with the flick of a wrist. It's frightening. I can make or ruin a man's career with a yes or a no. I can have people exiled or pardoned. I can command an audience with anyone I please. Yet, for all that, I cannot make true friends, I cannot find true love. Everyone loves me, but I must in turn love no-one, for to love one is to deny love to everyone else." She stroked Marion's hair. "Your mother was one of the few people in my whole life I managed to love as an equal. She was only an opera singer, not even the best, but she was beautiful, so beautiful, that for the only time in my life, I felt what it was like to be second best. When I was with her, men would stare at her, not me, a most extraordinary experience. I cherished her in Vienna, but in Madeira when I was ill, I depended entirely on her company to make me well again."

Sisi ordered Marion to stand up, then sit down again.

"I can see the resemblance most plainly. How old are you?"

Marion told her.

"When I last saw your mother she was not much older than you. What a life she had. She did not know it, but I knew about her past in Russia and Turkey. My husband Franz had insisted on having the secret police investigate her and your father. We knew he was working for the Russians, but I also knew that your mother knew nothing of your father's spying." She turned Marion's head with her fine fingers and studied her profile. "I quarrelled with Franz about it, he wanted to have Olive sent back to Russia, but I would not allow it. When I separated from Franz, I took your mother to Madeira with me. She saved my life. I can never forget that."

The Empress took out a small locket from her purse, and opened it.

"There we are, both of us. I twenty-three, your mother a year younger. It was taken aboard Queen Victoria's yacht in 1861."

Sisi handed Marion the locket. It was a photograph of two young women standing arm in arm aboard a ship, laughing and joking with the photographer.

"It was taken by Prince Edward. He was a young silly eighteen year old then."

The photograph had yellowed with age, but the smiles of the two women could be made out plainly. They looked so happy. Marion handed the locket back.

"No, dear" insisted Sisi "keep it. I imagine

you do not have a photograph of your mother, do you?"

"No" replied Marion. In fact she had nothing of her mother's at all. The only memory she had of Olive Vanya was the vault in the convent graveyard, a white granite edifice that had always given her the heebie-jeebies.

"It was not by chance that I have met you" continued the Empress. "I was told that you were in Bournemouth staying with friends."

"You knew I was here?" Marion was bewildered.

"You are a celebrity, dear. We read all about you in the newspapers. The trustee lawyers told me you were here. That's why I sent Valerie over to speak with you, so that I could meet you."

"But why?"

"Your mother made me one of the Trustees of your inheritance. Most of it I might add was stolen from the Austrian government, for your father was very clever, and had ways of tricking people. Nevertheless, he invested it wisely, and it is a healthy sum. With all the controversy about you and the dead girl, I had to find out for myself if you were truly Olive Vanya's daughter."

"And am I?" Marion asked as if it did not really matter about the fortune. She merely wanted to know if she was Olive's child or Clarissa's, or even the child of some unknown mother.

"No question about it. You have the same dark eyes and hair, and you really are quite beautiful."

Marion did not know what to say.

"You still do not know who I am, do you?" the Empress smiled.

Marion shook her head. "A countess?" she guessed wildly.

"Empress Elizabeth. You were named after me..."

Marion's head swam the way it had swam many times before when she had been confronted by the unexpected. This time she did not faint, she sat demurely staring towards the sea, watching Valerie throw the rubber ball into the waves, trying to coach Heinz into the water to fetch it. He barked and would not enter the water, and as they delayed, the ball began to float further and further from the shore. Marion's eyes fixed on the ball, bobbing up and down. She began to feel like the ball, seasick and helpless, and at the mercy of elements beyond her control. Her life was changing unrecognisably, and unless she took control of it, she knew she would drown.

*

Sometimes a story cannot be fully told as it is not fully known. Sometimes we can fill in the gaps by making it up, but we can never explain everything fully, or convince others that it is the truth.

Therefore it is with some doubt that you will now be informed that the fourth trustee was Kamel Tapiq, Marion's brother.

Naturally, he was unable to come to London from Constantinople, partly due to distance, partly due to the political animosity between England and the Ottoman Empire, partly because he could not forgive his mother for abandoning him.

When we first joined the story of Olive Vanya in the back streets of Constantinople, being beaten by her master's wife, we were unaware that she was also a wife of Tapiq. She was one of Tapiq's many wives, and at the age of fourteen she had borne him a son, Kemal. When she ran off with the deserter Emil, she had left her son with the harem, for his father doted on him even though he had three other grown sons. It was the other sons who had made Olive Vanya's life in the Tapiq household miserable. Behind their father's back, they had sexually abused and raped her from the age of ten onwards, and even when he married her when she was twelve, they continued with their molestations. When she had become pregnant she had not been sure whether it was the master's son or his grandson, for the brother's, in particular the eldest Ali, had continued to abuse her when his father was out of the house. The other wives knew what was going on, but as they were subjected to similar treatment, they were all too terrified of the punishment of death for adultery to inform the master.

When Kemal was born, Olive knew it was Ali's. It was a mother's instincts to have the father of the child accept it as his own, but she knew that this was not possible. When she informed Ali that he was the father, he scorned her, and denied ever having touched her. The fear of having a second child prompted Ali to use her solely for anal sex. The younger brothers made her their sex slave. Once, when their father was away, they kept her in a cellar and went down into the cellar to urinate on her. That experience, had almost sent her mad, but she swore that when the opportunity arose, she would escape the Tapiq household, and at a later date have her revenge.

Once secure in Vienna, using Grigori's money, she had arranged for the murder of the three Tapiq brother's. It was quite easy to hire paid assassins. She had their throats slit. She spared their father, her husband, for despite the beatings he had given her, he had shown her kindness as well as cruelty. The grief of losing his three sons was punishment enough, for she later heard that he had turned white overnight. As for her own son Kemal, he became the heir of the Tapiq scent and perfume export business.

Now, aged thirty, Kemal had received a letter from Fletcher, Son & Fearnell translated into Turkish that named him as a Trustee of the fortune left to an unknown half-sister. He had asked Fletcher, Son & Fearnell if they could verify the girl's blood type so he could compare it with his own. They supplied the information along with a short biography about his mother, and it was the delay in Kemal's reply to the blood type information that had held up the convening of the Trustee meeting.

When the reply came, Kemal confirmed that he and Marion were the same blood type, and although he could not forgive his mother for abandoning him, he held no objection to his sister inheriting the money.

He declared that he was more than wealthy. His father had died ten years before, and he had inherited his considerable fortune. He ended his reply by saying he hoped to meet his half-sister one day, perhaps when relations between their two countries improved.

10

The offices of Fletcher, Son & Fearnell had been completely re-decorated. The pending arrival of Empress Elizabeth of Austria had been the talk of the staff for the previous two weeks. It had been inconvenient sharing office space with painters and decorators, but it had added life to a building that for the previous half century had hardly ever had a window opened.

Jonathan and James Fletcher, two brothers, had started out in business as shipping agents in 1820. During the boom years of commercial trade with India and China, the company had capitalised its own fleet of merchant ships and purchased its own office building. As a family venture, Jonathan's two sons (James had no children) had been groomed to take over the running of the company, but Jonathan Junior had been lost at sea while rounding the Horn. James Fletcher continued to expand his father's and uncle's company, until by 1880, having bought out a dry-dock company called Fearnell, there were two hundred employees in their various order, finance, and legal departments, and a further six hundred enlisted as shipwrights and crew in their fleet.

Grigori Shum had made use of their services while shipping arms on behalf of the Russian government to the Far East. It was strictly illegal under English law to sell guns and canon to Russia directly, but by shipping to friendly foreign ports, then reloading and onward shipping to Vladivostok, their complicity went undetected. The use of the Fletcher Line ships had been crucial in the Russian campaign of expansion in the Amur River and Maritime Province of Manchuria.

As a result of the successful campaign, Grigori Shum gained considerable financial reward and he had consulted with the younger James Fletcher about investing much of it in London.

James Fletcher the younger was now sixty years old. He was a kind-faced looking man with large grey whiskers and eyebrows that seemed to fly. It was he who had called together the various trustees of the Rostov estate. It had always been doubtful that Grigori's fortune would be claimed by anyone, for he had never met the Countess Rostov, and wondered what state of mind she must have been in before her death when she had instructed him (through his legal department) to put Grigori's estate into trust until her daughter was twenty-one. In normal circumstances the Trustees would have have been empowered to spend money on the child for her education and well-being, but the Countess had left strict instructions that the child was to remain at the convent, that none of the Trustees were to contact her, and that the monies were to be left untouched until she came of age.

As executor of the Countess Rostov's will (appointed as such as the Countess thought that he had been a good friend to her husband), James Fletcher had forgotten about the Rostov's entirely, when one day a junior clerk brought in a letter sent from Meath by the Reverend Mother Gabriella reminding him that Elizabeth Shum would soon be coming of age.

It had not proved too difficult contacting the Trustees, for they were all people of considerable importance in their respective communities. However, the death of Mr. James and the transfer of his trusteeship to his daughter; the subsequent dismissal of the Reverend Mother to the Congo and the appointment of Cardinal Newman; the unstable nature of the Empress; and the clarification of the blood type requested by the Countess's son in Turkey; had made the job of chairing the trustee meeting in his office a difficult task. The added misfortune of the 'Rostov Baby' murder, and the national publicity which had led to probing questions about how the Rostov fortune was amassed, had made what should have been a quiet meeting of wealthy, intelligent people, into a media circus.

Before the trustees arrived, a barrage of newspapermen blocked the entrance to his offices, to the extent that Fletcher sent one of his managers to round up a posse of dockworkers, to chase off the pressmen. Meanwhile, because of the publicity that surrounded the meeting, a crowd of several hundred women and men had assembled out in the street to catch a glimpse of the Empress of Austria and the 'Rostov Babe'. One of the reporters heard a bystander state that the Rostov girl was actually the Empress's own child, and wrote it down.

However, we will not stretch our imaginations to believe such tripe. Paternity had been established beyond any doubt - Marion was the real Elizabeth Shum, daughter of Olive Vanya.

So on a cold December afternoon, locked in the Fletcher, Son & Fearnell boardroom room with Alice and Henry James; Cardinal Newman and his Monsignor; Empress Elizabeth, Valerie, and pet dog Heinz; James Fletcher, his thirteen year old twin sons, Henry and Eric, his secretary, his accountant, and company legal advisor, George Cramm; Marion, dressed in a simple white woollen jersey and long white skirt, sat on a hard-backed chair with her ebony black-hair balanced in a bun on her head. Over the back of her chair draped a long black Kashmir coat.

"The provisions of the Rostov estate" read George Cramm "are as follows ...... the lands and rents pertaining to that part of London known as Notting Hill. Sugarlands, consisting of one thousand acres known as Golden Grove Plantation, Garden River, Jamaica. One-tenth share of all revenues of Juares Silver Mine, Potosi, Bolivia.

Ownership of chateau and five hundred and twenty acres of vineyards at Chablis, France. One quarter ownership of the Opera House, Milan, Italy." The legal advisor paused.

There was whispering in the room. The breadth and extent of the Count's investments surprised everyone, even the Empress.

"The Rostov Estate" the advisor continued "includes cash deposits to date totalling five hundred and fourteen thousand pounds, nine hundred and ninety-two pounds, and six shillings."

This time everyone let out an enormous gasp, not least Marion, who would have fallen off her chair had not young Eric Fletcher caught her.

"Are you alright?" he asked

"Yes, fine, fine ... thank you."

"Your Highness, your Grace, ladies and gentlemen" interrupted James Fletcher "if I could have your attention. The purpose of this meeting is two fold. The first is to establish that Elizabeth is the genuine heiress to the Rostov legacy. Are there any here who would like to contest the legitimacy of Elizabeth's claim?"

"I feel" spoke the Empress " that we are all in agreement that this is the true daughter of OIive Vanya. She is so akin to her mother, in looks and temperament."

James Fletcher turned to the Cardinal "Your Grace..?"

"I have absolutely no doubts that this child is the child that was born to the Countess Rostov in our convent. I regret there has been some mix up on the way, but I believe you are all aware of the circumstances."

"Miss James ..?"

"My brother Henry and I have concluded without any doubt that Marion Elizabeth is the child of Olive Vanya. Henry had the opportunity to meet the other Elizabeth, didn't you?"

"For the record of everyone here" Henry said "I found young Sissy to be a very nice girl, and I feel that the events of the trial have painted her as a scheming, man-loving vixen. I believe she knew nothing about her own paternity bar what she had been told before leaving Meath. As one of the trustees, the Reverend Mother had told her nothing until she came of age, and I find it very sad and unbearable that the Reverend Mother and Sissy were misled by Clarissa Blum. It has been well publicized that I was the murdered girl's father, something I found out after her death."

Suddenly Henry broke down into tears. Normally a man who showed little outward emotion, the thought of Sissy's violent death cut him to the core.

"Thank you, Mr. James" James Fletcher uttered in a quiet tone.

"Can I say something ..?" interrupted Marion.

"Certainly, child."

"I would like to say that everyone has been very kind to me. I now have no doubts that I am biologically the daughter of Olive Vanya, but the only mother I have known is the woman you know as Clarissa. I still look upon her as my mother, as Sissy did. As a

Christian I must forgive her for what she did to Sissy no matter how much I loved Sissy. I don't care about all the land and money you are trying to give me, for I have lost my family. Sissy's dead, Clarissa's in prison, the Reverend Mother is in the jungle of Africa!"

Marion jumped up, snatched her coat from the back of her chair, ran to the door and threw it open. The corridor was crowded with staff waiting to glimpse the celebrity guests, and as Marion rushed out, they stiffly drew themselves to attention and let her past. She ran down the stairs and out into the street, past the dockers and reporters, the crowd and attendant policemen, and ran and ran and ran through the busy streets of London. She lost herself in the crowd and wandered for hours on end until it grew dark. Exhausted, she sat down on the steps of Nelson's Column in Trafalgar Square and stared into the night.

Finally, she made up her mind. She would make her own way in the world. The fortune could go to hell. She would find a job. There were thousands of Irish in London. Maybe if she could discover where the Irish community lived, she could find lodgings, make friends. She did not need any help from the high and mighty. If they wanted the Rostov fortune they could have it.

She got up off the steps for it was freezing cold. It had begun to snow. She had no money, but she had an expensive coat she could pawn. She was tired of doing the bidding of older people. It was the '80's and it was a young person's world.

ROBBIE MOFFAT

The author was born and schooled in Glasgow. He took a degree in English language and Literature at Newcastle University. He began writing when he was seventeen and has a had a career as a poet, novelist, playwright and screenwriter. He is best known for his feature film work in which he is also a director and producer.

His prose writing as been overshadowed by this. He wrote his first novel when he was twenty two and continued to write novels for the next twenty years. None of them were published.

The rediscovery of his prose work has lead to a recent spate of publications that has lead to a resurgence of interest in his prose work.

Printed in Great Britain
by Amazon

61050356R00102